Drinking from a Tin Cup

by Katy Perry

Steele Publishing Company, Inc., Gardiner, Maine

Book design by Katy Dunton
Cover art by Charlotte Agell

Published by Steele Publishing Co., Inc.

228 Water Street

Gardiner, Maine 04345

This book is dedicated to
BERNIE
Who shared nearly 50 years of my life
and hundreds of these memories.

Foreword

Katy Perry is not a typical grandmother from Hallowell. In recent years, she has run a local craft store, provided newpaper commentary on life in Kennebec County, run for the state legislature, even traveled to the Central American nation of Belize to work in the Peace Corp.

These diverse experiences have shaped a unique perspective on the world closest to her heart---country life in Maine.

Her collection of short essays is a wonderful tribute to the simple life. The stories capture the unique flavor of the people, the lifestyles, the towns, the land, and the culture of our state.

This book is filled with authentic images of growing up, growing older, family, community, and the pleasures of life outdoors and in the home. Everyday experiences become rituals filled with beauty and magic and the wonder of human relationships.

The warmth and nostalgia that flow through these recollections and descriptions reflect Katy's passion for her neighbors and her home state. It was a real pleasure to pick this book up and immerse myself in the special world that is rural Maine.

I know that readers---young and old alike---will find that these stories strike a special chord with their own lives. Clearly, the characters speak to our experiences as much as they do their own.

For years, Maine has prided itself on a rich heritage of quality writers. Katy Perry continues that fine tradition with *Drinking From A Tin Cup.*

- - Senator William S. Cohen

Introduction

Tomorrow is the accumulation of our yesterdays. If you subscribe to this philosophy, then you believe that in each of us dwells the sum of all that has gone before.

It is difficult to separate the happy events from the unhappy ones since time blurs recollections. What does remain is the patina of life, all the things that make the life we live uniquely our own.

This modest collection of my remembrances does not presume to be other than the recounting of milestones that have colored my life. Neither spectacular nor amazing, they simply tell of the warp and woof forming the fabric of a Maine grandmother's years.

This offering was undertaken primarily to be part of the legacy left to future generations of the Perry family. It is my wish that in reading these small essays, others will know something more of the person who trod these paths, the person known as Katy Perry.

An Irish Grandmother

It all came back to me as I read a collection of Irish short stories. Mayhap my grammie was not from Ireland; but as certainly as the Devil carried off O'Flaherty, she was woven of the warp of the Emerald Isle. She enjoyed a morning "cup a' tae," which she drank in the comfort of her small regal chair by the warmest window in the kitchen. Not before, in all the intervening years, had it occurred to me that hers were mostly the way of the Irish—although the culture she knew was sifted through that miniature gem off the Atlantic coast, Prince Edward Island.

Grammie Kelley, or Little Grammie as I called her (to sign her differently than my father's mother, who was tall and willowy), was squat and buxom. Never did she appear below the stairs without her apon. (Yes, apon—the 'r' was not sounded.) She did her share of the daily tasks, but because of a bustling clutch of females in the house, hers were the quiet ones. She mixed the batter for cake, cookies, bread or pudding, stirring steadily and with great strength and endurance. The batter was turned over to her daughter, Rebecca, whom she always referred to as "woman". "Here, woman, that'll be about right." And right it always was. Right into the waiting pan and into the oven. Knitting was her pastime. She knitted socks for the men in the family, mittens for the grandchildren and mufflers for using up the scraps of yarn left from more sophisticated pieces. Nothing was ever wasted in the house.

As the first grandchild, I was often left with Grammie and my aunts. Beds were scarce in the small duplex, so doubling up was an acceptable way. Because of my size, I suppose, I slept with Little Grammie, both at night and for the afternoon nap.

Once the kitchen was put right after the noon meal—with older children back at school and fathers back at work in the nearby mill—the three of us climbed the stairs. Big Grammie went to the third floor by way of a small dark alley leading to the second flight. Her age won Little Grammie the small diamond-shaped bedroom next to the bath. The furniture

1

was sparse. A high, three-quarter bed was pushed close to the outside wall, leaving just room enough to get to it past a tall bureau at the side of the door. In front of the bed a low chest held all the amenities of her toilette: a bold black comb, a brush, some hair pins and a small box that held a broach—a gold circle ornamented with a bronze maple leaf of Canada. Her rosary hung from a hook nearby; and just under it was a lovely glass receiver, the cover of which was open. Here Little Grammie placed the stray hair she had gathered from the comb and wound tightly into a ball.

It was not easy for a five-year-old to settle down after a heavy dinner—the noon meal was the "big" one in those days. Besides, with two bodies in that nest of feathers, it was a task just staying on top. The Big Ben with huge numbers ticked loudly and intrusively.

To me, the warmth generated by the enveloping mattress and the warm, lovely-smelling body of my companion brought sleep. I must have needed it because I can't recall wakening first.

Finally Little Grammie stirred, then sat up straight in bed and smoothed out her hair. When she sensed I was awake she would look over at me. "Be a good one now dear; reach my comb there for me."

I quickly responded. Still sitting up, she combed the straight hair from her neck, from the sides of her head, all to the top, holding it expertly in her free hand all the while. With it all gathered, she wet the end of her fingers with her tongue and coaxed the errant pieces into the fold. Then with a deft twist the top bun was assembled and long silver pins skewered into place, securing the coiffeur. Little wonder she was experienced. When I was five, she was 79 and had been performing the ritual twice daily for over six decades.

After swinging her weighty body to the side, she dropped her feet onto the floor with the stockings and soft slippers waiting just where she left them when she disrobed before the snooze.

In good weather, the afternoon was spent rocking on the porch. From this enviable position, traffic was the pleasure of the day. Walkers stopped to pass the time; those rich enough to own a motor car (and in the 20s there were very few) waved merrily as they passed, going slowly enough to be recognized.

Whenever babies came to visit they immediately became Little Grammie's property. They were handed directly to her with little ceremony. She picked up the tempo of her rocking and lulled them into quiet repose with her rhythmic, "whisha, whisha, whisha," in cadence with the creak of the old rockers.

As the babies grew into older children, she still wooed them. Canada mints were her bait. Someone must have kept her supply constant — nestled in her apon pocket along with a well-used handkerchief was always a white Canada mint. On rare occasions it was a pink Canada mint — but always she had this bit of confection. Perhaps her loyalty to the land of the Maple Leaf prevented her from acquiring chocolate. Thank heaven for that. Imagine the condition of a Hershey bar in that environment.

Visitors, any size or age, quickly came under her spell. All, of an age to reason, were worked into a game of cards. Whist of an evening, Casino or pitch for a quick game; it was all the same. The name didn't matter — it was the sheer joy of handling the cards and the excitement of what each hand would portend. She played to win — and it is known that she was not above some slight-of-hand to assure the victory.

Thinking back, I recall the superstition in her makeup, not unlike the Irish stories that inspired this essay. She didn't like cats. She tolerated one if it wandered by, but in the home — never. And, long before I knew her, she decided walking on the ground was bad for her! She would descend the porch steps to the ground level, but there she stopped. Even to put trash in the can, she would hand it to another for the few steps beyond the porch. What caused this strange habit no one has successfully explained, but it was her practice. Holy water was always available for special blessings whenever a fearful condition warranted, but a churchgoer she was not. Was it tied in to her reluctance to cover the ground up the hill to Mass? She encouraged all to "keep the faith," but a practicing Catholic she was not.

As I grew older I began to wonder about her earlier life. The story was told that shortly after she married, her husband went to sea and never returned. Even records in Freedom, PEI do not mention his or Mary Ellen's early life. A few years ago, I went to Lot II, a political division of that island, determined to learn what I could about my antecedents. Rather than being reassuring or revealing, it widened the gap between known and unknown.

The records at St. Bridget reveal that when my grandparents were married my grandmother's name was Rebecca O'Meara — and not Kelley as I had always supposed. The questions tumbled one after another in my mind. They never have and perhaps never will be answered. No matter. The important things remain.

My great grandmother, Mary Ellen Kelley — or O'Meara — was a staid and dependable lady, devoid of anything that could be called frivolous.

Her one hundred years were spent with a closely-knit family and a small circle of friends from the Island and her adopted United States. She was never known to look back nor to grieve over things beyond her reach. She led a simple life with few material pleasures. She never read — perhaps she could not — she encouraged ambition in her grandsons but felt it was ridiculous for the female to look for more than the roles of wife and mother. Despair was not in her nature, but neither was mirth. True to her Irish nature she would not risk God's wrath by laughter and smiled only rarely.

For whatever she was, I still sense her influence. A simple nuance in a Gaelic tale sends vibrations of her through me. She had to be Irish to the core. She had all the talismans of the nationality except drink. Never did I know her to imbibe even a sip. More's the pity. If she acquired all the other traits, it's too bad she was denied (or denied herself) the simple pleasure of a quaff among friends.

They Gave Christmas Away

Ethelyn and Richard Stubbs found it easy to be charitable. It was not only at Christmas that they shared their good deeds, but at that time their good deeds took on a more elaborate effort. This was the case in 1934, and surely time enough has elapsed to speak of their generosity.

Richard Stubbs was a popular Augusta physician. His lovely wife Ethelyn Burleigh told me at one time: "I was walking down Hartford Hill one day and this handsome young doctor drove by in his carriage—right at that moment I knew he was the man I would marry!"

With their comfortable home and well-stocked pantry, they both felt the need to share with those not so fortunate. It was mutually decided their gift to each other would be to give some family a Christmas they might not otherwise have.

People with honorable intentions can be as devious as those who are corrupt, so it was not hard to locate a family in need, the number and ages of children, their sex and clothes sizes. Once they learned all these facts, the very best part of the Stubbs' Christmas began.

Mrs. Stubbs did not drive and the dear Doctor did (often to the horror of pedestrians), so they shopped together.

First clothing for the little girls—from undies to warm winter outerwear—then the same for lads in the family. Clothes for the mother and the unemployed, ill father (perhaps the Doctor learned of the family as he tended the father) were the next purchases.

Shortly the dining room at 33 State Street began to look like a department store. Garments were labeled and piled together for each family member. Each week during the early part of December, the Doctor and his good wife drew the curtains in the bay window and put aside their usual evening engagements. They chatted and giggled over each garment like school children. They were joyously happy.

Visiting friends often cast a questioning eye at the pile of gifts that grew daily in the corner. Politeness prevented an open question. The couple offered no explanation.

Arrangements were made with a local dealer to deliver fuel to the family — a month's supply — and with the grocer to arrange everything for a sumptuous Christmas dinner.

When clothing, food and warmth had been arranged, there was still, what seemed to them, a need. Toys. Even with only one grown son, they realized that for children Christmas is the unexpected toy. During the final week they again took their list and went to complete the Christmas gift to themselves.

Finally they had to take someone into their confidence. They needed a taxi driver who would deliver the giant bundle of gifts, but one who would forget the address of the givers. Even this task was completed in secrecy.

The taxi arrived shortly after dinner hour on December 24. The gifts filled the car and trunk, leaving only room enough for the driver to struggle behind the wheel. Once the taxi was packed, the Doctor and his wife stood in the chilly winter air and watched the cab pull away and disappear north on State Street. Shivering a bit, they returned to the empty dining room with their small green tree on a table by the window. They pulled the drapes open and snapped on the tree lights. Each picked up a book and settled into their favorite chairs.

They had kept their pledge to give Christmas away. They had spent abundantly and had just sent it all away in a taxi, to people they knew only by name.

You may wonder how I know of this well-kept secret. I lived at 33 State Street in 1934 with my mother who worked as a cook for the family. I knew nothing of the preparations as they took place. Years later mother told me how she had shared in this beautiful story. In telling it, I hope some member of the Christmas family will finally know of their benefactors, and how each gift was wrapped with love and joy.

Percy Cain — Painting the Essence of Belize

Hanging over the table on which my typewriter rests is an oil painting of Belize City. It has magnificent blue skies and bunches of bouncing clouds dramatizing the sky. A palm tree lined canal cuts across the foreground of the work. A series of working boats with short wooden masts are tied up along the waterway. Government buildings and the Bliss Memorial Library occupy the background. Proudly waving atop the buildings is the Belize flag — a pennant that, when I look at it, brings a big lump into my throat. For you see, as loyal an American as I believe myself to be, I confess a fierce love of that country, where I lived for two hot years.

Percy Cain painted the work. Percy — who is not particularly well-known nor whose work is greatly favored in the country — for my money, does remarkable artistry. He makes his living as a carpenter and steals time away whenever possible to follow his more important talent.

When I first was in Belize, I saw some of Percy Cain's work and determined to own a piece. Not only is it fine art, it also captures the real essence of Belize. The time sped by amazingly quickly, and it was not until four months before coming home that I seriously began seeking his work. I found him one day far from the city working on a house remodeling. Thank heaven for a Peace Corps bike, otherwise I never would have reached him. I told him my mission.

He told me, "I rarely have work for long. I don't turn out much, but it usually is sold within weeks. Right now I am completing two oils. If you would like, I'll call you when they are finished."

That was a fine arrangement and I waited for the call. When it came, I returned to the work place. One quite large canvas was a river scene with women doing laundry in a northern river. The second was a nice painting of an inland waterfall. Both quality works, but neither prompted me to "own". So I thanked him and went on my way.

A few days later, I took a citation to a framing shop to be mounted. There I saw this striking oil of something with which I readily identified. I knew this was the work I would take back to Maine. Artistic and literary license has its merit. The painting I own is unquestionably Belize City. Cain has cleaned up the Canal and given it the majestic blue it should have, but which in real life is mud color and most unappealing. The way I want to remember it — beautiful, shining and lovely with flamboyant trees in full bloom and gulls sweeping around the boats — is the way it looks in oil. During a long evening, I look at it lovingly and wonder when I will return.

I guess the truth of the matter is, if you leave your world behind you and take up residence in another culture, it naturally becomes a part of you. I don't mind that a bit.

I am glad I was wise enough to carry home a painting of such quality, one that is a constant reminder that there are other places on earth where I can hang my hat and feel as much at home as I do here in Maine.

The "Good Neighbor" Policy

A few weeks ago I was unpacking a box of things that had belonged to my mother. Among other "stuff," there was a navy blue Georgette dinner dress circa 1929. It had all the flair of a Clara Bow outfit (remember her?) I tried it on. Darned if it didn't look a lot like a fashion ad I had seen in the morning paper. Let's see. That was nearly 60 years ago and here comes the flapper fad again.

Yes, things that go around come around (as the ol' feller says); but one thing I wish would reappear more often is good neighbors! When I was a child few mothers worked, so there was always someone in the neighborhood to "sit" if a parent wanted a day away — or a weekend, yet. This luxury is no longer around. Neither that extra egg nor cup of sugar to finish off a batch of cookies is attainable. Do you feel comfortable going across the street and asking to "borrow"? You probably don't even know your across-the-street resident. Too bad, isn't it?

I lived in the country many years ago, and was alone with two small sons throughout the day while my husband was at work. The neighbors we had were not really handy, but were the best kind of people to have available when you needed them.

Eddie and Dora Jackson, both gone now unfortunately, kept occupied with their small farm and family, and we did not neighbor as often as you might think. One summer afternoon a severe lightning storm whanged away overhead and I was less than comfortable in my ledge-based house. A rap on the door startled me. It was Eddie. "Dora says you don't like thunderstorms, Katy, so she sent me up to set with you through this one." How's that for a neighbor?

Another time, the boys were rigging the fishing pole to try their hand at the local stream. Somehow the barbed hook caught in the fabric of the chair, and in trying to free it, Paul pulled the hook through his finger! I was panic stricken. Paul could not free himself from the chair — and I had no idea what to do.

I sent Peter scurrying down the lane to see if Eddie was home. He was. Once he appraised the situation he went directly to my husband's tool box, found a pair of wire snippers and quick as you could say "Thank God," nipped the end of the hook off and freed Paul from the hook and the chair. That was not enough—he popped Paul into his truck and sped him the 12 miles to the Doctor's office in Jefferson for treatment.

These might seem extreme cases; but there were other friends throughout my life who shared garden flowers, fresh veggies, baby-sitting chores, a willing shoulder to sob on when calamities struck, and who were simply there when you needed them. I have been more fortunate than many—I have always lived in a place where people were friendly and talked with each other. There were no fences except to keep animals contained. Nowadays, fences seem to set people apart.

One of the motivations of Peace Corps Volunteers is to show people of other countries that Americans are friendly, warm individuals who truly care about others. It's a "Good Neighbor" policy that by and large is effective.

A friend's obituary appeared in the Bangor paper recently. Bob McKay was quite an amazing man who had gone back to college after his only child left home. The announcement further describes his personality: "Instead of sending flowers or cards, make friends with a stranger or shake hands with a newcomer in your town."

Bob McKay, Eddie and Dora Jackson were the kind of people to live near, if you could arrange it. But perhaps the most important way to find a good neighbor is to BE ONE! How long has it been since you took the time to reach across the back yard and chat with the lonely widow who lives there? Try that for openers. It will amaze you how good you'll feel about yourself when you get back home.

Finally, it's kind of hard to communicate with people from another culture and a different language when we fail to communicate with someone who speaks our language and watches the same television shows as we do.

My Grandson David

January is the birthday of my grandson, David Vincent Perry, age 12. Yesterday I mailed the eleventh issue of his birthday letter—hoping it would arrive in time for the family celebration. This idea began when I thought about his first birthday. Many things had happened during that twelve months—not the least of which was a hernia operation when he was only weeks old. That event alone, I reasoned, was excuse enough to set things down for future reading.

David's mother, Mary Ann, is one who loves nostalgia and family ties, so she encouraged me (it did not take much) to pen a yearly recount of family events. So it has been, and it amazes me the years have flown so fast and been so kind to the Perry clan.

Just before Christmas, I called to talk with the Massachusetts-based family. After wishing all the joy of the season—because we would be separated in miles, but not in love—Pete said, "Hold on Mom, David has something to tell you."

"Grandma, I'm going to Space Camp!"

"Space Camp, David—what is that?"

"Well, it's a camp where we learn all about space and have a simulated 'lift-off' just like the real one."

"When, David?" I asked, thinking it would be a day in the country.

"It will be during April vacation. I will fly to Atlanta with a lot of other kids and spend a whole week."

The reality of the situation is slowly coming into focus for me. Here is a grandson, a 12-year-old, fifth grade student already stepping into the world of tomorrow and the unknown realm of outer space. It blows the mind of his grandmother, who still has real difficulty believing that giant jumbo jets actually lift off the ground and fly thousands of miles aloft. It's probably early conditioning.

David is an average kid. He is prodded to do his homework, asks "what' you having?" when invited to dinner and gets along reasonably well with his younger sister—unless she becomes too pushy. His parents, however,

11

have always encouraged his interest in astronomy, magnets, science, hamsters, turtles (he has taken the class turtle for all school vacations) and every aspect of aerodynamics he could understand. In truth, his motivation to read was simply to entertain himself with science fiction stories.

So now he has been selected with a group of similar students from the Boston area for this exciting learning experience. I am thrilled the opportunity has come to him; and just as impressed that somewhere the word is out that future scientists—and, I hope, future environmentalists—must be nurtured early. When a kid shows interest and is thirsty to know "why," it's the right time to grasp the moment and build on that fragile curiosity. For too long that unique interest kids have has been overlooked.

David shares his birth date with Cyrus Ladd McLaughlin, a grand old man who was my stepfather. He died in 1964 at the age of 95—having lived a quiet, rather uneventful life, but having left some wonderful memories for my children who knew him as their only grandfather.

David is 12, Gramp would be 120. At least five generations in this one span. From Gramp—who told stories of his great-grandfather returning to China, Maine following the revolutionary battle on the Plains of Abraham in Quebec—to David, who will attend one of the first Space Camps for kids.

We DO build on lessons from the past. My prayer is that David's generation will lead the way in building PEACE and living harmoniously on this earth.

Happy birthday to David and all the other young space cadets celebrating birthdays in January.

Memories From Over Fifty Years Ago

It must be that the old brain has just so much room to fill before it over-flows, why else can I easily recall events of fifty years ago and find it difficult to remember a person's name from yesterday? I'm convinced there is so much trivia packed away in the cranium that the latest additions have no where to go. This simple fleeting thought from a few days ago set me to remembering the past.

There was a rather attractive, tall, athletic lady who lived on the so-called Medway Road in Millinocket. Mary is the only name I recall — except she also received a nickname from townspeople. It was "Bicycle Mary". She preferred the locomotion of her own peddling to that of an automobile. It was nearly two bumpy miles from her home to the downtown part of the town and she wheeled it all the way, no matter the weather. I have often wished I knew more about this lady, who dared to be different. "Nice" ladies did not bicycle in those days — and she did anyway. I admired her even then.

In the 20s, my father owned a Chevrolet dealership and a garage. He often was asked to drive "sports" from the B&A railroad station to one of the outlying fishing camps in the Maine woods. I was about six when he invited me to go along on one of these missions. At the time he was using a long, open touring car with isinglass curtains — in case of bad weather. The ride from Millinocket to Togue Pond, something like 18 – 20 miles, took a long time in any weather. Flat tires were common, and in the rain it might turn out that you simply couldn't get there at all! This particular day the weather was fine, and we merrily rolled along dodging boulders and ruts with fairly good speed. After discharging our passengers and saying goodbyes, the lovely lady who had been my father's fare came back to the car and handed me a shiny new ten cent piece. I recall the scene vividly even 62 years later — figure that one if you can. Even more startling would be if today's child considered a dime worth remembering for a minute.

In my youth, Uncle Eddie was one of my most favorite persons. He was horribly crippled with arthritis — he carried himself bent double and inched along when he walked. As Mother's youngest brother, he made his home with us for many years and I loved to hear him tell stories and jokes. One day he read an ad and chuckled, "New fall suits — I wonder how far they will fall?" I thought that the funniest statement ever and I flattered him by laughing wildly. And he was also a practical joker.

He visited Canada during those prohibition days with a friend. While gone — and, I suspect, under a mist of Canadian "juice" — he wrote mother a card announcing that he had bought a dog. Mother was in the cellar doing the wash when the mail arrived, and she was quite incensed that he would presume to bring a dog to our household without her sanction. Quite simply stated, she was furious and was prepared to give her brother a piece of her fury when he returned a few days later. He did return and no mention was made of the recent purchase until the proper welcomes were accomplished. Finally mother could hold her peace no longer.

"Where is this dog you wrote about, Eddie?" she asked coldly.

A wide grin lighted his face. I just knew that he had won a round. Slowly he reached into his pocket and withdrew a small, bronze replica of a bull dog and handed it to her. Mother smiled good naturedly — but knew she had been bested again by her cunning sibling.

The best thing about memories, I guess, is that you can toss away the unpleasant and keep the good things you want to recall. I have never had to work too hard to follow this practice — remembering only the happy past seems to come naturally — and it is, I feel, a blessing.

Rufus Porter—Yankee Artist

If you have never heard of Rufus Porter, it's not surprising. In simplest terms, Rufus was a painter, decorator, inventor and founder of the prestigious magazine **Scientific America**, still published today. The reason he might be better known in the future is that walls he painted in a Winthrop house are an important part of a new exhibit at the Maine State Museum. But first, a bit about the man.

Rufus Porter was born of prosperous farm folk in West Boxford, Massachusetts in 1792. He received part of his early education at Fryeburg Academy in Maine. He was quite a musician and earned much of his way fiddling. His father thought this a waste of time and apprenticed him to a shoe maker—but this situation didn't last long. Rufus was a wanderer and fiddled his way on foot throughout much of New England; in fact, along the Atlantic seaboard to Virginia. He lived the life of a migrant worker until his death at 92.

He was not so migrant that he overlooked family. With his first wife Eunice Twombly of Portland, whom he married in 1816, he sired ten children. Eunice died in 1848 and the following year he married Emma Tallman Edgar of Roxbury, MA. In 1859 his last child, Frank Rufus, was born.

To provide for his family, Rufus played violin and flute at fancy dances, painted drums and sleighs, traveled aboard a trading vessel and painted at ports of call, did portraits and cut silhouettes. During his travels he perfected a camera tool that aided portrait painting. With this adapter, his paints and other gear on a hand cart, he traveled about a completely independent man.

One of the house murals painted by Rufus was well known to Winthrop people. The house had been a private home, a hardware store, a hospital, a lawyer's office and a cabinetmaker's shop. It finally housed the Lewiston, Greene and Monmouth Telephone Company which sold the property to an Augusta bank. The miracle is that the painted walls remained and that those interested people brought the fact to the State Museum officials' attention. The building owners, the bank and the Museum cooperated to save this valuable historic and artistic piece of Americana.

Rufus Porter was a man far ahead of his time. The freedom he demanded throughout his long life must have been a hardship for his family; but, in his roamings, he perfected an impressive array of talents.

I suspect he would have been deadly bored by our talk of him today. He might well have retorted, "I am just doing what I enjoy doing. No need to carry on about that."

Note: The walls from that Winthrop building, so carefully "dropped" and preserved in the early 1970s, are now part of an exhibit at the Maine State Museum. This display is just off the lobby of the museum and was opened to the public in early 1989.

Dedicated Friends

Ruth and Lowell Baltz were Peace Corps Volunteers in Belize while I was there. We entered the P.C. together and took our training in Miami. I would find it difficult to name a more delightful couple to be with, no matter what part of the world I was in.

Lowell had been a high school teacher, and after two dozen years behind a desk he wanted a change. Ruth, who lived her beautiful life as a wife, scout leader, 4-H leader and mother, and who was happiest making her man happy, quickly agreed to apply for a Peace Corps assignment. Their life together was a model of what a marriage should be and certainly an inspiration to all.

The summer of 1988 when they returned to Wisconsin, Lowell was delighted to find employment at Yellowstone Park — a job he'd always hoped for. But remember that summer? The sweep of fires throughout the park kept all their friends concerned. We didn't know if they were in fire danger or not, and letters to them were not answered. Around Thanksgiving, I decided to treat myself to a phone call to their home, not knowing if they would be there or not.

It was like finding a treasure when Ruth answered the phone shouted to Lowell, "Come quick! It's Katy Perry, calling from Maine!" We had a fine chat and I was relieved to hear that although they had indeed been in the thick of the inferno, they were not in great danger at any time.

Just before Christmas, I received a sizable packet in the mail. It was a copy of the log Lowell had kept during a 14-day stint at a small woods cabin at the southeast end of Yellowstone Lake. I read it with the same interest I had read an autobiography of John Muir a few years ago. Lowell, an ardent naturalist, knows the names of flora and fauna and truly has an impressive regard for the environment. If feel certain he would approve of my sharing some of his comments with those who read these lines. Few of us surely would know such an experience — or would want to!

"August 27, 1988 — Five of us +100 gal. of pump fuel and 30 gal. of torch fuel got aboard a ranger boat and 45 minutes later were at S.E. Arm

17

(of the lake). The radio said the fire was about a mile from the cabin. The Ranger stayed out in the lake and said over his loudspeaker, 'The whole side of the mountain is on fire!' All I could see was smoke.

"September 1, Thursday — We've been here a week. I was up first and walked along the shore after a morning face wash. After another week will be due some R&R — but for me it will be S&S (soap and shampoo) — Our crew chief has a portable radio on at all times. — They expect the North Fork fire to come right over Elephant Black Mountain, I may be in for more fire-fighting than I thought.

"Sept. 2 — All afternoon a steady breeze blew for smoke cleared enough to see a mountain to the east we didn't know was there and by the bottom a small fire. Within a half hour a huge wall of flame put on a spectacular show for us.

"Sept. 3 — See my last comment. — We are now threatened by it — less than a half mile away."

During the following days Lowell was up early, walking to vantage points to watch the fire's progress and to write his thoughts on paper. I have been impressed with his comments about the experience, his ability to identify the kinds of trees that were torched and the bird calls he heard, and the identification of animal tracks he saw around the area. Although it was bear country, he did not see any — but probably realized they were as intimidated about their habitat as the fire fighters were.

On the final day Lowell's comments were, "While waiting for the helicopter, I hiked north and saw how the fire had come through. Really complete burn-out, not 150 yards from the cabin. Put out a few spot fires near the cabin. Art said, 'Let them burn' but one was in a thick stand of spruce and I didn't feel like pushing our luck. Help finally came — we could see where the front ran up the mountain and which way it was going — this tale may not be over yet!"

Meantime, Ruth was back at their home base wondering if her husband was alright. These two fine people continue to dedicate their time and energies to making the world a better place for today and future generations. I feel genuinely favored to count them among my friends.

Grammie's Kitchen

Grammie's kitchen in the small Maine town, like many during the Depression years, was neither pretentious nor unusual. For Grandmother, like other housewives of that era, chose kitchen tools that were completely useful, practical and simple. There were no matched sets of anything. The cupboard held just that—cups and saucers, plates and tumblers. The carpet was not indoor-outdoor, but well-worn-in-the-middle and patterned-around-the-edge Congoleum. In fact, a youngster of today transplanted back 60 years would surely question the things there. You might even question some things. Let me tell you . . .

A rickety porch boasted two well-worn rocking chairs (each logged a thousand swinging miles a season). Only two giant steps across the porch put you in front of the kitchen door with its peeling paint and brass doorknob. The door latch was low enough to be handled by a child. If the knob was turned and the door swung wide, you were confronted with the entire room. From here the tour begins.

A chair by the door has a mate just beyond a low, oilcloth-covered table. These are set in front of a window modestly covered with a lace curtain (a bit of shanty Irish, melad!) This was a pleasant arrangement. You could sit and drink afternoon tea with a caller, lean an elbow on the table and see people passing by. It was a perfect place to pick up the deck of cards always resting on the window sill and while away the time with a game of Ol' Sol. Then, too, if a caller should come in, the cards made it handy to suggest a game of pitch.

To the left was the heart of the kitchen—yea, the heart of the house, the Home Comfort. The black iron range turned out baking soda biscuits that you would think were made in heaven. No one ever fussed over that stove as people in this day might. It was meant to serve, and serve it did. It warmed in winter and cooked to perfection. It heated the water for all purposes and dried socks and mittens (or more delicate garments on rainy and snowy occasions). For all the things it was capable of doing, it needed to be fed. Dry soft wood for kindling the fire; heavy, cumbersome hard wood to maintain it and for baking. It fell the lot of all small tykes to keep wood on hand! "Emptying the ashes" was rather objectionable, especially on a windy day. The ashes, of course, went into the garden.

Except for the large pine wood box set safely back in the far corner, the wood was stored in an outside building. In that day, the woodsman did not deliver wood to the house as the oil man delivers today's fuel. He brought the wood, but chances are it was in long tree lengths. In Gram's case, there were no men around, so several neighbors would spend a couple of Saturdays with a "borrowed" saw-rig and saw the long wood into "stove lengths". I don't ever recall money changing hands for this service. A helping hand was considered her right as a widow. Those who have never heard the whir of a saw as it bites into wood on a crisp October morning have missed something as basic to a wood stove as the lid hook — and more's the pity!

A tall galvanized cylinder stood just to the right of the wood box. In some more prosperous kitchens, this cylinder was copper; but Grammie's served the purpose. This was the water tank. Coils in the fire box of the stove heated water from the tank and gradually the entire 25 – 30 gallons were bubbly hot. After a long Saturday of baking beans and bread with the stove humming all day, the tank would start cracking and clanging. That meant the water was too hot. There was nothing for it but to run off some of the hot water to cool the tank. This would be the time for Saturday night baths. Come to think of it, cooling the tank might be the reason Saturday night was such a popular time for sudsing.

That is how water was heated at my grandmother's. It might just as well have been a large tank built right into the end of the stove. This arrangement was double trouble. Not only must the tank be filled with cold water, but the hot water had to be dipped out and dripped across the room to the sink for dishes, laundry or the bath tub. This water situation went on forever and ever. Now we feel greatly favored to have hot water from the tall tank by simply turning the spigot in the sink!

The icebox looked straight at you as you came into the kitchen from the porch. It was made of wood, zinc-lined, with a single door that opened in front and a hinged door that opened on top. There was room for about half enough food. Most of the upper portion was needed to store the ice that the iceman brought in 10-,15- and 20-cent chunks.

The icebox seemed a device for keeping kids out of mischief. As the ice melted (newspaper was carefully wrapped around it in summer to lengthen its life), the water ran down a tube to a hole in the bottom of the chest. A makeshift container collected the melted water. This collector did not come with the ice chest — it had to be improvised. It was the child's responsibility to keep watch and empty it before it overflowed. It seemed the pan always needed attention during a game of "caddy" or tag. It was tricky, I can tell you, moving a flat pan of water safely to the sink. If a thin line of water began to snake across the floor, we ran with a mop to clean it up.

If there was anything of value in Grammie's kitchen it was the clock that sat on the shelf over the icebox. An oilcloth ruffle around the shelf was the only decor in the room. Special papers that came in the mail, the pay-weekly insurance book or a grandchild's school paper — might be tucked behind the clock for safe keeping. The ticking clock kept company with the snap of the fire, lending a complement to family conversations. Never intrusive, just comfortable.

Now for the sink. The long, black iron sink never — I repeat **never** — had dirty dishes stashed away in, beside or under it. The sink was empty, except right after a meal or when a basin was placed in it to "rinse out a few things". With the dishes washed, dried and put in the cupboard or back on the table ready for the next meal (as was the way), a sheet of newspaper was crushed up and used to wipe the sink free of any splashed water. If dry, the iron sink would not rust. As a child, I reveled in being the first to run more water into the dried sink and see the rivulets meander toward the screen in the center.

Just above the sink were racks to keep the dish towels and dish cloths handy. Beside them attached to the wall was a soap dish, a wire enclosure on a handle where the remains of bars of soap were deposited. When vigorously shaken in hot water, the wire dish made soap suds. The results: the early relatives soap powder and detergent.

Over the sink and around the third corner of the room was the dish cupboard. There were few family treasures, but what she had was housed there.

A second window provided light for anyone using a well-padded rocking chair. Little Grammie Kelley sat here to stir a cake (she invariably sat to complete this domestic act), knit a pair of wool winter socks, or rock a visiting grandchild. Beside it was a "work basket" with needles, thread

21

and scissors for mending and replacing lost buttons. Very little extraneous material in this kitchen!

The last wall supported a two-sink, soapstone "set-tub". The name describes the use. Clothes were "set" to soak in one tub, then scrubbed on a scrub board after the grime had been loosened in the soaking. Scrubbed and wrung out by hand, the garment was tossed into the second tub where fresh water was used as a rinse. After thoroughly jostling them around, they were once again wrung dry, shaken, trotted out the door to the rickety porch and hung on lines. It was often necessary to duck the clothes when coming or going. Double caution was needed when the clothes were frozen stiff during winter months.

It remains only to speak of the roller towel on the back of the porch door. A long length of crash cotton was sewn together to make a circle of material. Placed over a removable rod, the towel could be used for several days. Rotating allowed one area to dry while another area was used. Really cut down on the laundry. During slack seasons, the towel might go for a week! During mud season — never more than a day.

That's how the kitchen looked. The wondrous aromas from that kitchen were something else. The smell of strong black tea, fresh bread, steaming camphor oil, and "yellow" soap all mingled together to create an indescribable odor — but one truly distinctive and worthy of a story by itself. The human flavor of the place was equally distinctive.

In Grammie's house, friendliness was abundant. There was a welcome cup for neighbor or stranger. Compassion was ever-present. A collection for the church or for a family in distress, a word of medical advice or an impromptu visit to a sick bed, a kind word for someone needing it or a sharp rebuke when it seemed in order — all of these came forth from the ladies of the house as the occasion demanded. Gaiety was spontaneous. A good chuckle was easy to invoke, and a bit of Irish wit was as natural as life. It was a good place to be, that kitchen. A fitting reason to refer to those as the "good old days".

I would have to say that kitchens without Grammies to work them would not be worth calling the days back. The best we can do is remember. If in recalling it makes us happy, then the days were fair ones and worth the living.

To Keep Or Not To Keep

As cozy as I am in my one-bedroom nest, some days I pine for an old farm house with a massive attic, a dry warm cellar, and several barns with lofty lofts. You see, I am, as if you haven't already discerned it, a collector. Too much, far too much, of too many things.

I have tried to reform. A few years ago when I decided to leave the country for two years in the Peace Corps, I wallowed through furnishings, linens, books and artful pieces gathered during forty years of homemaking. I could not bear to touch the accumulation of papers. They are still with me; and although they do not take nearly as much room as dishes or tables or chairs, they need storing to say nothing of culling.

A few days ago, I was asked to find a photograph of a friend's wedding. The fact that the wedding took place in 1941 gives you an idea of the sifting I needed to do. For two days I have been at the chore and still no photo. What I have found is three large boxes filled to overflowing with memories. How can I let go such a vital part of not only my life, but the honest core of who I am? It is a rank fallacy to believe my children will have the same feeling for this assortment as I do—yet there is some measure of proof that things of value may exist in the pile.

For instance—letters from Charles Savage, a man of unique talents who owned Asticou Inn in Northeast Harbor. A man who designed the magnificent doors for Thuya Gardens in that Mount Desert town as well as the gardens themselves. An accomplished musician, a person with impeccable taste in decor—a man who flattered me by asking my advice on a furniture purchase when I was a mere college freshman. And there are notes from a lecture by "Bucky" Fuller, materials and photos from the celebration of the V.A.'s 100th anniversary, and story notes from dozens of people I interviewed at the historic Augusta House when I aired a daily interview show. The list goes on, and although it might not impress you, I feel there are some things of historic note.

23

Recently I read about and joined a group of people discussing the letters of a lady homesteader. The letters spoke intensely of life in the early 1900s in Montana. Letters in my collection from my young husband stationed in the Pacific during World War II surely will have meaning for future Perry generations, if not historians.

So how do I store all this and still have working space at my desk and bedside? Carefully, I guess. The biggest problem is having to sift through everything just to find one item I need. Not only does it consume hours of time, but it awakens thoughts—ideas long buried in the rush of today's tasks. Letting these questionable treasures go is something akin to losing a bit of one's self. I'm simply not going to do it. Just this minute I have resolved—they stay with me. Another generation will have to make the decision to chuck the lot.

When I go out this afternoon, I will go directly to an office supply house, buy a small filing system and spend the very next rainy day once again sorting, filing and preserving. Then I am going to wait for Mary Ann to visit.

Mary Ann, the truth should be known, is a more avid collector than I am. She comes from a long line of collectors—her mother, a delightfully talented lady from Indiana, has taught Mary Ann all she knows about saving and storing, so Peter's wife has already been given the burden. It will be this lovely daughter-in-law who must decide.

She will be with me a week or more, and I will lower the boom. We are kindred spirits already, and I feel secure in the knowledge that she will think no less of me for the responsibility. Fact is, Mary Ann will probably welcome the filing system as much as the papers. She has plenty of her own to add.

Best of luck, dear #2 daughter!

Ma

In another essay, I spoke about good neighbors. That piece has been nagging at me ever since. Each day I think of another wonderful person who has brightened my life and from whom I have learned many important lessons. Such was Emma Chase.

Emma followed her lumberman husband, Harry, from New Hampshire with her babes. After they took up residence in Whitefield, the family brood swelled to five sons and three daughters. I suppose when the boys grew and brought home prospective brides, her name gradually changed from Emma to Ma. At any rate, for the last 55 – 60 years of her 95 she was known affectionately by friends, family, neighbors and absolute strangers as "Ma". It fit her perfectly. Here was a woman feisty and determined, outspoken and opinionated. What might be termed negative characteristics were so softened by caring and courage, warmth and generosity, they were soon attributed simply to being Ma, the unique person she was.

My oldest son was just over six months old when Bernie and I bought the five-bedroom farm house in which Harry and Emma had successfully reared their brood. The house was big and roomy with a delightful view of the spire of the Whitefield Church peeking through the trees along the Sheepscot River. I had no ambition to duplicate their family number, but I remember being morally supported by the thought that I was following in the footsteps of a most respected lady. She proved a fitting mentor, and came to my rescue more times than I can count. She was on hand for parties, for accidents caused by small boys, when babies would not stop crying, when I needed a recipe or when I hungered for some woman-talk. Somehow Ma always had time to spare for a person in need.

This story is told about life during the Depression when most of the family was still at home. A wood shed jutted off the runway to the attached barn and privy. Harry and his lads spent most fall afternoons splitting and storing the winter wood. Certainly for the boys it was not a labor of love, and it's pretty certain this end of logging was not a favorite of the man of the house either.

At any rate, it was cold, windy and unpleasant on the day I am speaking of. Ma had her ingenuity pressed to the limit finding food—and enough of it—to feed her gang. When the time came for supper to be served, she opened the back door and shouted to the workers, "Supper's ready, come on in!"

The men kept working the wood. After ten minutes or so, Ma again swung open the door and sang her song, closed it with some force and returned to her tasks. The pile lowered; and though the boys were ready to call it a day, Harry wanted to finish the job—so they stayed in the shed.

After another ten or fifteen minutes passed, the lady of the house stormed out to the shed, hands on hips. "Didn't you hear me? If you don't get in there right now, your suppers will be cold as ice. Now move!"

Harry seldom countered Ma but this time he dropped the ax, looked right into her eyes and exploded, "For God's sake, who in hell ever heard of bread and molasses getting cold!"

It was serious business that day, but the story of those times has lighted family gatherings ever since.

One of my favorite memories of Ma happened on a snowy winter morning. My youngest son was only about three months old. For four days and nights I had fed him, warmed him, rocked him and performed every task that had ever soothed the first three. Not Andy. He kept crying. Calling the doctor was expensive, and I doubted if there was really anything truly wrong with the child. I went to the phone and called Ma.

Before long, she and Harry came trudging through deep snow banks up the hill, impassable by car, and walked through the door.

After a quick once over, Ma turned to me and said, "You nursing that kid, Katy?"

When I answered in the affirmative she asked, "How old is he now?"

"Three months."

"Are you giving him anything else to eat?"

"No."

"Well, for heaven's sake, Katy, that kid has had enough slop—give him some gut-wadding and see how he does!"

I fixed a small dish of cereal, fed him and Andy dozed off to the first uninterrupted sleep in nearly a week. So did I.

Ma Chase—one of a kind. A real Yankee good neighbor.

Parenthood — Firm But Loving

What kind of parents would let their six-year-old son go off to a neighboring city for a day dressed in one gray sneaker and one black sneaker, one high-top, one regular? Wonderful, caring parents, I say. Parents who see their child as an individual with designs of his own, who do not set up road blocks at every pass — parents that every child should have.

I confess that was not my mode of parenting; and I suspect others — or at least those of my generation — felt the overpowering need to have their children "conform," with never a thought that they were stifling imagination, self image or creativity. Today — too late and far more pliable in my appraisal of what is "right" or "wrong" — I applaud, yea, wildly applaud the parents who allow their children to make such major decisions for themselves. Major decisions such as the kind of footwear they will wear.

Such a set of sage parents, and Isaac's parents qualify, DO make such decisions. Such as supervising what their child watches on television or telling their child that the pet is a little boy's responsibility and he will tend its needs. Such decisions, I suspect, are handed down in a manner that is not demanding but quite acceptable to the youngster.

Ah, yes, the joy of parenthood carries a gigantic responsibility. Just as the saying goes, "It's lonely at the top" (I think it was Harry Truman who said it), being a parent is also a sometimes lonely, self-agonizing job. Harry had major decisions to make that affected the nation. Parents have to make decisions that affect a developing human being — when to be firm, when to be soft, how to show love when you are undeniably angry. The role is complicated. The wonder is that so many do the job so well.

Several years ago, I visited the daycare classes at the Capital City Regional Vocational Technical Center and watched Jane Harvey with her small brood of youngsters. Jane — who has since gone on to a position where more children will benefit from her amazing insight into child development — treated the children with calmness, obvious love and firm discipline. The kids knew what Jane said and knew they would obey. This

27

is a simple statement, but the results evolve from a step-by-step, day-by-day process that begins with the first encounter.

Let's go back to the odd shoe family. It happens that the father of Isaac is a poet. He is also one of the most mentally agile, charming young men I have met in years. The following poem I found delightful; and, as one not fond of rhyme, such fare may change my mind about poetry.

What We Did Today — for Isaac at Four

I know someday for you these moments
will be extinct like the dinosaurs
We play with on the livingroom rug.
The climate will change, something
inexplicable will happen, layer upon
layer of experience like silt will
bury your memories. Each day you learn
more and more, how to plant seeds,
how to pump on a swing, how to ask
questions no one can answer.
All day we play together.
I become a sleeping giant, you a
fossil. We become faithful
companions, a cowboy and his horse.
You feed me imaginary oats after
our journey into the kitchen.

At night you call me into your room.
You say you need water, you need to
pee and in the middle of the night
you need to whisper something to me,
a secret you say. And you press your
lips so close to my ear that I can't
hear what you are saying, I can only
feel your hot mouth, your lips as they
move. I am naked in the darkness at
the edge of your bed, listening to the
mystery of your breath, you who came
from me, cell upon countless
cell. I think how each of us

begins there, cells like the
first cells of everything that
has inhabited the earth, even
your dinosaurs, how we have all
arrived from that moment,
how we are evolving, slipping
away.

Stuart Kestenbaum

Phyllis Hanley — No Nonsense, But Special

Every person, I suppose, knows a special older person. Mine lives in Gardiner and is named Phyllis Hanley. In the 20 years I have known her, she has always been the witty, efficient, no nonsense lady she is today. At first meeting, I came under the spell of her infectious chuckle at the Maine Heart Association. Her chuckle and her peppery eyes still work the same magic and always delight me.

She was born Phyllis Brown and, as she tells it, was brought up by grandparents and aunts. Whoever was responsible, they nurtured a balanced personality who shows tolerance and joy in the smallest beauty, a lady who surely is making the world just a bit better and — because of her passion for plants and flowers — more beautiful for her presence.

The wit that is Phyllis' second nature is one of her most charming traits. A case in point: When I first went to the Heart Association, I was unfamiliar even with the workings of a copy machine. Phyllis had taken my work several times and copied for me. Finally one day, she said, "Katy, come out here and let me show you how this machine works." I did.

"Lift the cover, place the paper to be copied like this, see?" she began. "Now all you have to do is punch this button here, and they tell you to count backwards from ten. When you reach one your copy is ready. But I've found if you time it about right, you can get in a whole "Hail Mary" at the same time! Much more sense to do it that way, doncha' think?" Productive and practical.

A few weeks ago I was thirsty for some time with Phyllis and her style of humor. We went to lunch together. The conversation was of many things, for Mrs. Hanley is vitally interested in local history, people, writers — well actually, everything in life interests her. We spoke of age. That sent her into a recounting of a telephone call the night before.

"When I answered the phone, a very pleasant-sounding man asked me if I was happy with the delivery of my TV Guide. I said it came regularly and I had no problem." Then the following conversation between Phyllis and the salesman proceeded:

"Well, Mrs. Hanley, at the beginning of the year we are going to raise subscription prices. However, as a special 'preferred' [!] customer, you can remain one of our favored clients at the same cost, if I can sign you up tonight for an additional two years. How does that sound?"

"It sounds very good, but, young man, at 81 you must know that I am not about to sign on to ANY special for two years. In fact, I'm not even sure I'll be here until next October when my subscription expires."

No hostility, no nonsense, just plain honesty. That's Phyllis.

When I drop her off at home, I carry for hours her sense of fun and interest in life. She is a refresher. I need Phyllis' levity and keen analysis of living. I treasure the hours we spend together and scold myself that they are not more frequent.

Gerard Hanley, Phyllis' devoted husband, passed away some years ago. If there was ever a married couple who enjoyed each other's company, it was the Hanleys. They had their ups and downs, to be sure; and Phyllis is as apt to say how angry he made her as she is to remember the times he got up to adjust the TV set, and stopped to kiss her cheek before he sat down. A simple act of love — a conditioned response — as natural and right as their love for each other.

Phyllis Hanley is no "goody-two-shoes". She has her human frailties as we all do. It's just that for me, she is special. I want her to know that on my charm bracelet of friends, she is one of the brightest gems.

Water From a Tin Cup

The other night I had fish chowder for supper and found it had made me thirsty. I reluctantly left the most exciting part of a dandy story to trek to the kitchen for a glass of water. Instead of reaching for a tumbler, I took the tin measuring cup from the dish drainer and filled it with cold water. Instantly I was back on Uncle Edgar's rickety porch in Brownville.

Never has cold water tasted so good as that I drank from the pump on that porch. There was a round-bottomed tin cup hanging on the porch wall handy to the pump handle. Everyone who needed a drink used the same cup. It was not very sanitary to be sure, but whether the cup or water — that taste has lingered favorably for decades.

As I sopped up the water the other night, lots of other memories from another time raced through my mind's eye. Aunt Pearl. She was Uncle Edgar's devoted wife and my mother's older sister. They never had children and were kind to tolerate me for a visit now and then. Edgar Glidden was a gruff old fellow — for he must have been well in his 60s at that time. He was small and wiry and demanding.

"Don't slam the door when you go out," "Shut that door quick — you'll let in a house full of flies!" are things I remember of him far more than anything else. I wonder if he would be offended that this is how I recall my visits. Children DO have retentive memories.

Aunt Pearl's house was immaculate. The floor was such, as they say, that you could eat off it. She had interesting decorative pieces here and there — things I wanted so much to feel and even take home — but I did neither. She was a tall lady who wore quite stylish clothes for the community in which she lived. She dressed for afternoon rather than simply removing her apron — I suspect some very young people reading this (if such there be) would question what an apron is! And what a cook. Her doughnuts were marvelous. No one sampling her fried doughnuts would tolerate the Dunkin' kind.

Perhaps my brightest memory of Aunt Pearl is her funeral. It was the first I ever attended; and to this day I can see the parlor stripped of all furniture so that the friends and family gathered there could be seated to listen to the local parson offer the eulogy and listen to the congregation singing her favorite hymn while her dearest friend played, very badly, the hymn on a foot-pumped organ.

Oh, dear—that was almost 60 years ago, yet a cup of water from a tin cup sweeps me back through those long years. The Gliddens impressed me. I would like to believe I learned something from them both. Patience and caring for others from Aunt Pearl—for she tended friends all over town when there was need. From Uncle Edgar—I trust his lack of humor and this demand that a five-year-old follow his directions just as he laid them down—made me realize how very difficult it is for youngsters to obey all rules. But he was a good, kind and generous man.

Now I've told you all this, I'll get another cup of water, slide down in the easy chair and spend another dozen minutes or so remembering Brownville, Maine and the white clapboard house on the side of the hill where I spent some weeks a-growing. I hope you take some time to relive another era now and then.

Hot or Cold — A State of Mind

After a pile up of consecutive days of torrid temperatures, a cooling trend and the threat of thundershowers were welcome predictions. People's tempers caused outside chores to suffer. Hardly anyone wanted to do anything.

Now it will sound unsympathetic if I tell you a lot of the lethargy is in one's head! The heat, for sure, was real; but dwelling on it and the discomfort it brought was not a whit lessened by complaining. I admit, quickly, that people with respiratory disorders or malfunctioning thermostats HAD to take care — but I'm speaking about the average Joe and Jill who find discomfort as readily with the cold. My theory is "go about your business, think as little about the heat as possible, drink lots of liquids and keep your mind c — o — o — l." Honest, it works. The difficulty is trying to isolate yourself from the myriad of others who are not about to give up the complaining.

I am not a superperson, but there is something to be said for one's state of mind. When I was accepted into the Peace Corps three years ago, my assignment was two years in Belize, Central America. The climate in this small subtropical land boasts an average temperature of 79 degrees and an average humidity of 85%. That's average, mind you. There were days, and even months, when the temperature and humidity reached the 90s with no relief as the sun went down. Often the breeze died down while the temperature stayed the same. Having read all about this in publications the Peace Corps sent to orient me, I made a real determination that I would "cope". I realized it would be hard to adjust — and indeed it was — but I trained myself to accept the heat, the humidity and all the other things I would be expected to endure. For the first two months — September and October are wretched — I fell into bed in the early evening completely

34

exhausted. The climate took a toll, but slowly I began to adjust and the next 22 months were not bad.

This may sound like a lot of ballyhoo to you—and I grant you your two cents' worth—but I really think setting my mind into a grid of acceptance of whatever came my way worked. I wasn't any cooler, I found my shirt soaking wet at 8:30 in the morning when I biked to work, I found it almost impossible to turn over in bed because I was stuck to the bedclothes in perspiration—but I managed. It worked for me.

Last winter, my first back in Maine after two years in Belize, was the most wonderful winter I ever remember. It was a treat to be cold. You can put on lots of clothes to get warm, and the cold is invigorating, Perhaps that's what we should be thinking about during the hot days of summer, and recalling those hot days might warm us when the snows and storms whistle around the eves this winter.

One of the great things about the State of Maine is the diversity of seasons we have. It's a sure bet that if the weather does not suit you today, it most certainly will tomorrow.

Norlands — Living History Everyday

One visit to NORLANDS LIVING HISTORY CENTER some years ago convinced me I wanted to return for another visit, perhaps a "sugaring off," or a more extensive tour of the facility. It was not until I read a piece in **Maine Say**, the newspaper for readers over 55, that I determined to join others in a jingle-bell sleigh ride.

During January and February this year, the winter rides were planned for Saturday and Sunday afternoons — a perfect time to make the outing a family affair, for surely every kid should have at least one ride wrapped in a warm robe behind a pair of energetic horses.

There had been a luscious snow fall earlier in the week, else the going would have been rough. The ridge on which this preserved farm is situated was a picture postcard scene as we took off through the woods behind the little school. Each horse wore a bright brass bell, and we made a merry sound as we rode along. Kids, parents and grandparents rolled together in the hay — some of which kept us company the rest of the outing (hay does cling).

As much fun as the ride was, it was equally as interesting to me to chat with the farmer-like young men who drove the horses or thrashed the beans in the farm yard. Norlands is a working farm. The cows must be milked, the chickens must be fed and watered, and the stoves must be stoked. It is, in fact, a step back in time to visit and see something of how life was lived a hundred years ago in Livermore Falls, Maine.

If you are new to our state, you may not know that Norlands is the birthplace of the Washburn brothers. These seven young men left Livermore after their schooling and carved a place for themselves in the history books of the United States. They brought a giant kind of fame to their native state as well. Much gratitude must be given Billy Gamage and her valiant volunteers for establishing a foundation to protect and preserve this set of buildings for Maine and future generations.

You may be interested to know that Elihu Benjamin Washburn, who was born in 1816, graduated from Harvard Law School, established a successful law practice in Illinois, became a U.S. Congressman and served for a time as President Grant's Secretary of State before leaving to become minister to France. And he is just ONE of the seven!

Another interesting part of Norlands is the farm library. It seems there was interest in having a building near at hand to house the accumulation of reading material the family assembled. Face it, a group of people who made such an impact on the world HAD to be readers. Well, it seems the person responsible had visited the charming Hubbard Free Library in Hallowell and wanted to duplicate the structure just south of the house. It was done almost to a "T", using granite quarried in the Granite City along the shores of the Kennebec. That building, the main house, the big barn and the school building across the road form the major part of the farm.

School children probably know more about this center than their parents, but it certainly is a place to see at any time of the year. For more information about special events or scheduled summer classes write: Norlands Living History Center, R.D. @ Box 3395, Livermore Falls, Maine 04254, Telephone 897-2236 or 897- 4918.

Happy Memories of a Three-Day Sail

❦❦ It's not unusual to have people join our cruises from Ohio, Utah, California and other states; but we love it when a State-of-Mainer comes aboard," Erma Colvin said. Erma should know. For the past eight years she has been chief cook, happy receptionist and sometimes deck hand aboard the *Isaac H. Evans* out of Rockland. Her comments were an offhand welcome to join a three-day cruise on this graceful windjammer with trusty Captain Ed Glaser at the helm.

If ever you can forget about fancy duds and pancake makeup, it's aboard such a vessel. What you need and ALL you need is a set of warm, waterproof clothes and a change for warm sunny days. In fact, the smart sailor puts all essentials in a small pack and with a multitude of plans for a do-nothing, relaxing sail, is off and away.

Most people think windjammers are all based in Camden. Not true. Five of the wonderful flying boats are berthed at the North End Ship Yard in Rockland. This is toward Camden from the Maine State Pier. I went aboard on Thursday evening. We got a warm, but unceremonious welcome. A Northwest Orient Airline pilot, his attractive stewardess wife (aboard the same plane) and their fourteen-year-old son were sitting on a bulkhead talking with Captain Ed. The tone of the next three days was set right there.

It's remarkable how well things are planned and secured on a boat. Space is adequate, but that's all. Beds are comfy with plenty of blankets to keep out the cold and dampness. The toss-up is, should you hunker down to get into the lower berth or climb to the upper?

Of the three days we had one of sun, one rain and one fog—about average for the coast of Maine. To be sure the rain and fog are not as enjoyable as the sun, but each element brought beauty and memories to savor. There was wonderful wildlife to keep interest high. We spotted ospreys, a couple of bald eagles (some with binoculars spotted nests), seals and porpoises. Plenty of diversion to overlook the weather, and constant conversation among two dozen individuals all interested in each other, defeated any thought of boredom. It was heavenly respite from land-based tensions.

One unexpected member of the crew, Captain Glaser's eight-year-old son Daniel, lent nothing but charm and diversion. This curly-haired youngster is a real charmer. Extremely knowledgeable about almost any subject, he is a card shark, a raconteur (his dad cautions that Daniel is not always to be believed— "He has a treacherous imagination," he said), and about as safely independent as any child I have known. It was obvious that he had been schooled in the do's and don'ts of sailing and never was he cautioned, told to put on socks (it was c−o−l−d) or told to eat! He just seemed to do all the right things, which led me to wonder if we don't sometimes talk children into disobedience.

The last day out, we awoke to a heavy fog. This was not surprising— we had anchored and gone to a small island the evening before for a traditional lobster bake and paddled back to the *Isaac* in a cloud of mist. It proved to be a damp homecoming; but fortified with many cups of hot coffee, it was great. Daniel, however, had the best of it.

About the time we got underway, he strode down to the cabin he shared with his dad, trailed a dark blue blanket back to deck, perched himself atop the 7-man raft and, snugly wrapped in wool, curled up and slept all the way home!

Getting underway is exciting. Erma piloted us out through the first thin passage. With teenage agility she hopped into the yawl boat, started the motor and as soon as all lines were cast off, eased the towering "mother" boat away from the wharf. As we moved away I had the sensation it was leaving us, not the other way around!

Once out in open water, sails hoisted with amazing grace (something like the gospel song, to be sure), we floated free from the tethers and gave over to the wind. It was delightful!

A sail, even for only three days, makes one realize the importance of cooperation. Impossible it is to fetch cups and plates up the galley stairs. Another pair of hands is necessary. "Tacking" or "coming about" takes acute timing, strength and willingness to take orders. Cooperation. It's important in all walks of life. In sailing it is mandatory—windjammer sailors seem to have it without resistance.

Almost every adventure in life is reckoned by the food served. No problem aboard the *Isaac Evans*. Three far-more-than-ample meals kept guest and crew satisfied. The meals are planned (by this I mean purchased before sailing, stowed and iced if necessary) and prepared and served by Erma.

The meals were perfect for the occasion. Hot blueberry muffins, scrambled eggs, bacon, juice and plenty of rich, perked coffee set us up for the first day at sea. So many sailors who have eaten Erma's meals insisted she write a cookbook — darned if she didn't do it. **Schooner Fare** outlines menus for a week's cruise (some recipes based on serving 26) and contains the "how to" for each dish with charming illustrations by artist Lynn Travis, herself a windjammer cook from time to time. The book is available dock side or from the *Isaac Evans*.

Highlights of three days at sea? The beauty of the Maine coast — its hard, cold beauty unlike the placid, undramatic Caribbean. The instant thrill of spotting seal loping near the boat. The joy of people. They come in all shapes, sizes and from all walks of life and parts of the country. Each, given a chance, has a story to tell and something that a listener can learn.

Perhaps my favorite memory is of Captain Ed and his son. Daniel had just come up from below deck. His father was occupied with a nautical maneuver at that moment; but, seeing his curly-haired prototype emerge from below, he left his post momentarily and clutched his son to his chest in a deep, loving hug. It was a spontaneous gift of love. I'm glad fathers do that more today, and that they are still doing it when the child becomes a man.

Three-day cruises will again be available this fall after the week-long sails have ceased. What a glorious thing it would be to see New England foliage from the water!

My Ice Fishing Career

Years ago I found myself a smelt-fishing widow on many occasions. The colorful little communities huddled together up and down the river had always intrigued me. The cold, the treacherous slippery ice and the water's depth made me shiver, yet I was fascinated.

Often I suggested we find a babysitter so I, too, could go off to the ice to bait the wily, little silver fish. To say the suggestion was not warmly accepted by friend husband leaves a lot unsaid.

Persistence, however, is something I have a lot of. Finally we made plans to go as a twosome. I busied myself with warm garb, some finger grub (I was told that was the right kind) and engaged a delightful young woman to oversee the boys.

It happened the tide would be "just right" on that particular night at about midnight. This presented the first of many dilemmas. Did I have a nap before leaving, read until the appointed hour, or just stoically wait? I waited.

It did not take long to understand the social structure of a smelt shack village. The daily fishers knew all the angles. They could tell you the right place to chop the holes in your particular shanty, how best to start the fire, the exact (or so it seemed) way to hang the lines — these sages left nothing to chance. Pity the unwary smelts!

At the outset, it was steely cold in the shack. The sound of paper kindling small twigs was encouraging, as crackling wood seems always to be. In no time at all, the small enclosure warmed up and we began shedding our outer wraps — first the jacket, then the hat, then the outer sweater, then the inner sweater, then a blouse. But how far can you go — even with only your husband in residence? It got HOT, I mean H−O−T.

"Well, open the door if it's too hot," he said.

I did. For about two minutes the climate was just right. Slowly swirls of zero air lapped at my feet and the cold creeped upwards. My upper body was fine, but the lower extremities were not. I was too occupied with my body temperature to keep my eyes on the ever-important baited lines.

Once everything was in order, of course, my husband had to cover the ice beat to find who was catching what and in what amount. That, it turns out, is an important part of the ritual. When he left, I remained to "watch". Let me tell you, an inexperienced watcher hardly qualifies to be left in charge of such an important operation. I watched so intently that I became mesmerized by the swaying frame on which the lines were secured. That – added to the moist heat, the early morning hour without sleep, and just a drop or two of protection (against the cold) – did me in.

I dozed. First thing I knew I was slipping off the makeshift chair and sliding onto the ice – dangerously near the square icy hole! Just in time, I caught myself and quickly took up my post in the chair. And not a minute too soon. My husband came through the door with a couple of longtime friends he met on the ice. He brought them along to meet me – can you imagine? What you can't imagine was my complete relief when the guests began to leave, saying:

"Might as well call it a night. Tide's turned and no one has had any luck tonight anyway. Perhaps the moon isn't right. Don't know about you, but I'm for home. See you later."

After so many weeks pleading for a chance to go "smelt-fishing," I was not about to be the first one to suggest retreat.

"Guess Joe is right, hon. Might's well close shop. Why doncha' pick up our stuff and I'll load it into the car. I should be able to get a few hours sleep before I leave for work in the morning."

Admittedly, my ice fishing experience was about 20 years ago. Probably they have electric heat today and a hamburger joint near the village. At any rate I learned my lesson. I had enough of it on that one outing to last a lifetime.

Perhaps my husband knew full well that one time would do it, and from then on he could join the guys at the smelt shack village without having the little woman beg to tag along.

It worked.

A Christmas Story

Julius, a medical student from Lithuania, was spending his first Christmas away from home. Studying in Germany had seemed a good idea, but then the war erupted and everything became more difficult. It became more important that he finish and return home to help in the rehabilitation of his homeland—if the war ever stopped.

Christmas morning in 1944 saw snow spreading over the German landscape. It was cold with a sharp wind blowing. No bad weather ever kept this devout man from his religious obligations, and on this day he attended sunrise Mass reasoning he would then have the remainder of the day to study.

Following the service, Julius decided to walk to the outskirts of town and enjoy the beauty of the day before returning to quarters for a meager breakfast. He bundled his muffler tighter around his neck and pulled his wool cap down over exposed ears and set off at a brisk pace. The noise of the awakening city joined the crisp crunch of his boots on the cold snow-covered earth, and a Christmas tune sung by the church choir probably ran through his head.

His stride was long, and it seemed no time at all before he had left the village behind and was well on his way when a persistent hum crept into his consciousness. It did not disturb him, but as it grew stronger its source suddenly startled him. An airplane! Out of habit he immediately looked for shelter. Planes did not fly over this small community unless the mission was deadly. Not only did the thought alarm him, it also angered him that such a bombing run should take place on this holy day.

Julius ran ahead where a large tree offered some protection. He scanned the sky and spotted the aircraft, but it zoomed far overhead and quickly passed the place where he stood. He would not be a target—and, thank God, neither would the school. The walk continued and within minutes, the earth shook as bombs were dropped on a munitions factory known to be south of his location.

The sun was getting higher in the sky and Julius turned back. He would keep Christmas in mind, surely; but it would be easier not to think of the warm, wonderful Christmases back home if he buried himself in books.

He was approaching the street near the village square when that awesome buzz of an approaching plane returned. People scurrying around also heard the sound, and immediately a familiar sense of panic spread through the street. All looked heavenward. It was easy to spot — it was low in the sky. Surely there was nothing of importance to "bomb" in this university town — but reading the minds of American strategists was something no one was able to do.

Julius watched with the gathering crowd. Shortly they saw an object in the heavens. As it descended people began to guess what it might be. It swayed from side to side, so there was certainty it was not aiming for a target — so was not destructive. Suddenly a small red parachute opened, slowing the descent and straightening the fall. Hanging gracefully beneath the red canopy was a small, well-trimmed Christmas tree!

Now there was genuine excitement. Everyone ran to where it seemed the landing would be. People came out of houses and stores; and as the rush increased, a kind of joyful chatter broke out.

All eyes were guiding the tree to its resting place. It slowly came to rest almost in the exact center of the square — as if a giant magnet had attracted it.

A small note attached to one of the lower limbs of the tree read simply: "Merry Christmas from the United States Air Force."

There was a mingling of released tension, joy and thankfulness that brought a smile to Julius's eyes as he wiped away a tear.

Note: the name of the student has been changed — but the story is true. It was told to me about 25 years ago. The student finished his studies and emigrated to Canada after the war. Eventually he found his way to the United States, married a woman from his village in Lithuania, and together they raised three sons and one beautiful daughter who have each made positive contributions to this country.

Annual Pilgrimage to a Winter Beach

It might startle you to know how many people walk the beach in winter. It doesn't surprise me, because I'm one of them. Almost deserted, the beach, when the cold winds whip off its icy shore, has much to recommend it. New Year's day is a favorite time. This year, 1989, New Year's day falls on Sunday — a perfect time to pack a thermos of hot soup, bundle up in warm gear and waterproof boots, pack the kids and the dog into the family car, and head for Reid State Park or Popham Beach. If you can squeeze another item in, add a kite and really let things fly.

For several years this has been a mini-ritual among my small group of friends. Edith loves to pack lunches. I loathe the idea of preparing food. Emma, the amenable soul she always is, will bring dessert, two thermoses of coffee or a flask of wine. Me? Well, I prefer to do the driving as my contribution to the day, and each of us seems to be satisfied with the arrangement.

We meet at a mutually agreed-upon point, and giggle about family happenings all along the way. You see, this is a "catch-up" outing, for we don't often see much of each other during the summer. Once we arrive, we pull wool caps over our ears, don an extra pair of mitts, tie scarves tightly around our collars and step out into the breeze. If the wind is strong, as it is apt to be, we bend against it on the way over the sand dunes to the shore. Once there, we keep the conversation to a minimum as we set out at a brisk pace.

There is little need to keep together, so we go at our own speeds. A fault of mine is to look for small treasures tossed up by the tide. A bit of smooth, water-washed stone or wood is something I have a hard time leaving behind. Now and then it may be a sand dollar I covet, but it could be as insignificant as a colored piece of beach glass. The other troopers are far more select in their acquisitions, while I am happy with mine.

Our timing is pretty good. It's at about the same moment that chilled fingers and icy toes suggest we retreat to the vehicle to the goodies we know await us. The walk is usually at a slower pace (hard to work those frigid limbs), but the frivolity has not lessened. We chuckle over our finds, delight in the capering dogs taking a New Year's bath in the undulating waves, and marvel at the infants snuggled against their moms' warm backs as they greet the New Year. People of all ages, we see, enjoy the beach in winter as much as we do.

Steam rises from the thermoses of coffee as we snuggle into the dash board lunch counter. We find it a task to break a tuna sandwich in two with refrigerated fingers. A piece of fried chicken tastes heavenly washed down with piping hot coffee (we should be most thankful for such a worthy invention). And that splash of brandy does sharpen the brew's appeal.

As we eat, we enjoy the arrival of other brave souls starting their new year right. There is a camaraderie among winter beachcombers. We wave and chat together like old friends.

If the day has not been too hard, we may take another shorter tour of the beach; but usually we start back, allowing plenty of time to take side trips to a second-hand shop, to another point of land or to the houses along the way. Over the years we have had some pretty fascinating encounters on the return trip.

If you want to welcome the New Year, I can think of no better way than to get out into the cold, clear, sharp Maine air. See you at the shore on the first!

The Fearless Trio

We should have known better. Three brilliant (writer's opinion) retired ladies truly should have known better. It was not until we reached the midpoint in our adventure that the thought came we were skirting danger.

It was one of those remarkable days in late January. The temperature was balmy, the sky was brilliant blue, ice melted in rivulets making the ground soft and soggy. A perfect day for mountain climbing. After several phone calls we were off to Camden, Maine for a walk in Camden Hills State Park.

The parking lot was free of ice with black top exposed all about. Spring had come — and we might well have been the first fearless trio to take advantage of the situation.

Shortly after leaving the car we realized that not EVERY trail was free of ice. The way was slippery in some places, but we were not in the least apprehensive. A nearby trail seemed to have the right degree of difficulty to take us to the top and give winter-lazy flab a quick tightening up. Valiantly we sallied forth. Ignorance is not always bliss, it is also foolhardy.

We had not gone more than a quarter-mile when the trail (really a wide route between trees and, thankfully, well marked with a white blaze) shot straight up into the air! We stopped and speculated about the incline, but decided we were up for it. We overtook the hill magnificently, if I do say so myself.

It was around just another bend that we met the glacier. Rain, sleet and melting snow had joined forces to create a sheet of beautiful blue-white cascades of slippery cover — a space we needed to cover if we were to reach the pinnacle. Another stop — another decision. This was probably just the accumulation of water coming to the bottom! We would find the going better once we passed this point. Traipsing far to the left of the slide, we clung to trees and shrubs and slowly gained the top. As we proceeded, we decided we would certainly walk down the road we believed was on the opposite side.

Alas, the way did not get better. It got steeper and more slippery. Reasoning that we would have an easy time of it once we reached the top, we continued.

It was tough climbing, but each of us commented we could feel the air getting thinner and the light at the top brighter—we were going to make it.

An hour and fifteen minutes later we did. Betty was first up and instructed us to plant the flag.

"We're here!" she shouted.

"Do you see a road down?"

"Nothing but rocks."

As soon as the rest of the party caught up with her, we walked out onto the ledge and beheld a perfect view of Camden, the harbor and the road south toward Rockland—but absolutely no road down. A nearby sign stated we had climbed Mount Megunticook, which was 1 mile—not the 6.7 miles we had speculated.

Our only options were to follow a sign pointing to Mount Batty (which we looked down on from our vantage point) or return the treacherous way we had come.

Good judgment suggested we follow a known route, as precipitous as it was, rather than attempt the unknown again.

Except for knees that buckled, slippery leaves and the ever-present ice, we descended far more quickly that we has ascended. I dropped to my knees several times from slick leaves, but was not injured. My companions stayed upright, but we all admitted to pretty shaky limbs once we reached the bottom.

Dumb luck brought us back to the car. If any of our children had even thought of such a venture on January 31 in Maine we would have read them their rights; but we, who should have known better, set off in ignorance of the terrain, never once considering what any one of us would do in the event of a broken leg or a twisted ankle.

Now that the adventure is over, we are smug about it. There was a moment or two as we clung to a steadfast pine tree when it was not a bit funny, but we learned a lesson so not all is lost.

"That will be a hard act to follow, doncha' think?" Norma said as we waited for a bowl of hot chowder in a Camden restaurant.

Watching Children Go To School

It was one of the simple joys of my mother's life to watch her grandsons trudge off to school. Their mother was far too preoccupied with boots and mittens to see the joy of the event. Today she does.

I am fortunate enough to live on a street near the elementary school in Hallowell. Daily I listen for the shouts of kids on their way to class. A look at the clock reveals the unholy hour they must arise to prepare for the day. Often it is just after I have left the warmth of my night's lodging; and I shiver for them as they journey into the winter winds. Forty years ago, getting tots up, fed, dressed and out the door was commonplace. There was certainly no time to be concerned for one's own comfort or the trauma of those kids stepping outdoors; and in that day it was not to wait for the bus on the family porch. They had a long trek down an often snowy country lane and a bone-chilling wait for the bus (believe it or not, there WERE school buses at that time).

The kids I watch these days are lucky, I think, to live near enough to have a short walk to school. They are awakened with a sting by their morning walk, and surely will be alert for the studies of the day. In addition, they get an unsupervised look at life with their peers as they traverse hither and yon. The street sings with their noon-time trip back home for lunch.

Often there are startled shrieks that bring me running to the window. Sometimes it is a small bully who has run off with a pretty girl's hat, or a miniature fist fight over who-knows-what. It is the dilemma of a small lad not to reveal his difficulty, but to persist in his pathetic sobs down the length of the street. It's all part of growing up, I guess; but it does keep a senior citizen's day from being dull.

As the children vacationed during the past holiday season, I missed their comings and goings. Now they are back, and snowballs sail through the morning skies after a storm. Little kids don't toss them high or hard, so window panes are safe.

It seems I have come around to my mother's way of thinking. Watching youngsters on their way to school is a joy. It brings a spot of life into the early morning. The red, blue and green mittens and scarves against the white background of snow create a mosaic that brightens up the day. Their animated shouts of youth affirm that deafness has not overtaken me. Life and learning is about the same as it was when I went to an unattractive brick building across the field back in the 20s, and when my two oldest sons hurried to the historic King's Mills school in Whitefield in the 40s. I was luckier than they — my building was warm. They often had to help the teacher build a fire in the big, round stove in the center of the room! The scene may have changed, often dramatically, through the years; but kids seem to stay about the same regardless of the generation.

Perhaps the difference is not in children, but in observers. We've changed and now see things in quite a different way than we did before. I thought one way as a student, another as the mother of students and yet another as a grandmother watching today's generation of computer kids. Each view has its good and bad moments — but isn't that true of life in general? The best thing, perhaps, is to enjoy each moment of each day from whatever vantage point we may have at the moment.

A Summer Evening's Walk

There's a wonderful feeling about lazy summer evenings. The day's work is done, and if you are one of those wise people who can turn the "off" button on the TV, there is a myriad of things to do. I like to walk. The pictures you envision of people who live in the houses you pass may not have any basis in fact, but I like to think I know the people by the place they call home.

The gardens are a case in point. One family will maintain an ambitious collection of perennials fastidiously tended. Nearby, another has a similar profusion of colors – not quite so tidy, yet there is a semblance of loving care in the placement of the plants that grow tall behind those that keep low to the ground. Husbands (we suspect) walking the to and fro of mowing the lawn, stop long enough to wave and offer a "good evening." In some cases the welcome is warm enough to brazenly stop for a short chat.

Rarely do you find the family sitting on the porch today; kids rarely play croquet in the yard or swing on the creaky hammock on the side porch. Such an evening arrangement used to be the perfect way to visit a neighbor. It only took a ten- or fifteen-minute stop to catch up on the latest family news and coddle the newest child. I suspect when the front porch was the meeting place of the neighborhood, there were community disagreements and personality conflicts; but it would seem the simple art of communication was better.

People who live near the shore or by the river – and those of us living along the Kennebec are truly blessed – have a unique chance to savor the beauty of the twilight. Have you ever noticed how much more intense the colors are just before sunset? It's my favorite time to look at trees and riverbanks and the sky. The evening sky is beyond description in its variety of rainbow colors.

The air is soft and friendly in the evening. The winds that bothered during the day have faded, and leave behind a gentle breeze so coaxing that I find it hard to go indoors.

At least a couple of days a week I like to walk around Hallowell, where I live. I take the hills going up and enjoy the bonus of the walk downhill after the climb. If my energy level is up to it, I walk the Litchfield Road or up Winthrop Hill to the turnpike overpass. It sounds absolutely silly — yea, even childish — but I get a genuine high from waving at the passing truckers zooming below on the highway. They always seem to see a person on the overpass — and almost always they wave. If they happen to pull the overhanging cord and send a blast of their trucker's horn skyward, I almost jump with joy. I hope my wave breaks up the tedium of their cross-country or cross-state driving as much as their friendly toot delights me. Truckers, I have always found, are about the nicest people on the highway.

Ah, yes, a summer evening, in Maine especially, is something to enjoy right up to darkness. Even as you return home and the lights begin to snap on in houses along the way, there is a feeling of coziness about it — home is where the heart is, sort of.

One thing about it: if you enjoy the twilight hours as much as I do, you have to catch every one you can as they go by. First thing you know you'll have to put on an extra sweater — the days are already beginning to shorten!

The Flavor Of Thanksgiving

It was legal in the early 30s to shoot deer, and if you were lucky enough, to bag a moose. Families during that decade literally lived by the luck of the hunter's foray. Hunting in those days was not considered a sport, but rather a way of life.

Ada Perry was always relieved when her son brought home the carcass of a game animal; and she, believe me, was not one to let any of the meat spoil. She knew how to preserve every scrap of venison that was in the meals she prepared for her family during the winter months. One of the delicacies she knew well how to "can" was mince meat. Apples newly gathered from the trees, suet — the fatty tissue near the loins and ribs of the animal — raisins, molasses and spices from the neighborhood grocery were all combined in the proper proportions and cooked for hours on the kitchen wood stove.

The aroma of this concoction was almost too tempting to live with. It was tasted by Ada, her children and any visitors so often, it's a wonder any was left to put away. But there was always plenty.

During the winter a savory mince meat pie coming out of the oven was ambrosia! But it was at Thanksgiving time that the first test of the fall labors was savored. It was not the norm to serve the wedge of steaming goodness with a dollop of ice cream in that day — for it was an ice-box, not a refrigerator, that kept family food. Often food was simply put in the back shed for cold storage — believe me, Millinocket, Maine in November boasted sheds cold enough to freeze the words in your mouth. The pie, covered with a crisp, flaky crust, was the perfect completion to the traditional dinner. Even stuffed to the gills with a sumptuous meal from this capable cook's hands, everyone eyed the remaining pie — just to be sure there would be enough for another wedge when no one was looking.

I remember calling on Ann Kelly a few years before she died at 101 years of age. This delightful lady was just taking a pan from the oven — and it smelled GOOD. My friend Madelyn and I waited until the deed was accomplished and then asked if we were intruding.

"Whisha, of course you're not," this Irish charmer said, "It's a TRY—PIE and I'll thank you to share the first bite with me!" You know that it didn't take more than one invitation to accept this generous offer. Ann went on to explain she always did a test run a few days after her mince meat had aged—and before putting it in jars. Best to be pleased with the mixture before the task was finalized. Madelyn and I placed our stamp of absolute approval on Ann's efforts and went home delighted we had firsthand experience of this autumn ritual.

Alas, it has been many years since I, too, carefully cut the meat from Bernie's trophy and made mince meat with apples from our Whitefield trees. Truth is, I miss the results; but honestly, I confess it was a chore to complete the process.

This year, Boynton's Market in Hallowell will supply several pies I will carry to Farmington to a family get-together, as I have for many years. Jake Baker and his crew are using a recipe for mince meat he acquired when he bought the popular Water Street store from Albert Boynton. It seems to come out right EVERY time and is as delicious as any mince meat I have ever eaten. This may sound like a testimonial for Jake's product and perhaps it is, but tradition does not have to be forgotten. If your early holidays included mother's mince pie, take a tip from me—enjoy it again this year with Boynton's Market doing all the hard work.

So let me wish each of you joyous Thanksgivings, and leave you with the words of Arthur Guiterman in his work, "The First Thanksgiving".

"So once in every year we throng Upon a day apart, To praise the Lord with feast and song in Thankfulness of heart."

Christmas — The Giving Of Ourselves

As Christmas approaches in late December, so does the winter solstice. Take heart — the hours of daylight increase once this day is past. We can look forward to a sharpening of the cold, but an increase of light!

But Christmas is my theme. Permit me, please, to share some random thoughts on this very special time of year. There are many manifestations of the spirit of the Christmas season in the most usual daily happenings. Over the years I have seen many.

It was in 1934 that Richard and Ethelyn Stubbs spent hours buying, wrapping, and delivering gifts of toys, clothing and food to less fortunate families in the Capitol city area. This quiet doctor and his stately wife performed their annual ritual in complete anonymity lest they be looked at as do-gooders or, even worse, bring focus on those they sought to serve. They, I believe, made their Christmas by foregoing their gifts to each other, but rather gave to others.

During the war years, I traveled from Milo, Maine to Guilford on the B&A railroad to spend the special week in a bleakly cold farm house among warm, wonderful friends. My husband and my brother were both holed up in the Pacific doing what soldiers and sailors were told to do. Our hosts, the Stones, waited each night for news from England to learn what they could about their son stationed there. It was not the happiest of times, yet we (my mother and I) were brightened by the hospitality of their home; and believe we, in turn, gave our hosts something more to think about than the awesome battles raging around the globe.

The bleakness of Depression years are, too, tucked in memory. A note from my mother to my brother John, explaining that Santa simply did not have enough sleds to go to all the kids that wanted them, satisfied him. "That's O.K., Santa," I vividly recall him commenting after I read the message to him. Children, given the chance, are really quite reasonable, I believe.

Christmas in Belize, 1985, was hot, humid and quiet. The Belizeans are very religious and use the weeks before the holy day to scrub every inch of their homes. They paint, paper and brighten as best they can. Christmas hymns booming through the open windows of homes and stores are a little strange when you are used to hearing them wrapped in a muffler, but are no less sincere for the temperature. I had been asked to housesit for a young man in the U.S. Embassy who went back to the States for Christmas, at a pretty palatial home compared to others in the city. It was near the church, so I walked to Mass in the heat of the early morning and met a small child crying on the sidewalk.

"What's the matter?" I asked.

"I'm hungry," he responded.

I questioned and got half-answers about his mother not being home, about the door being locked, about so many things that did not add up in my mind. It was Christmas and I found this condition particularly troubling. The best I could do was go back in the house, find some fruit and rolls and take them out to the bereft child. We walked along the street toward the church, hand in hand, and talked together. Along the way we met a small friend of his; and not knowing what else to do, I turned the child over to his friend—hoping that whatever the wrong was it would be easier to correct in partnership. This may seen a careless way to dispose of the problem, but it had been forcefully pointed out that visitors in the country NOT become involved in political or family conflicts. I calmed my emotions about the situation by remembering the child and his anguish in my Christmas orations.

You and I have had glorious Christmas celebrations; yet, if you look back, surely there were some less fulfilling than you wished. Since the very first Christmas it has been that way. I wonder if you may agree with me, in reflection—does it not seem that the sparsest celebrations were those that carried the most meaning? In truth, it is not the gifts of Christmas that make us happy, but rather the giving of ourselves and the nonmaterial gifts that most satisfy.

Whatever Christmas holds for you, I hope it will always be one of peace, joy and love—with just enough gifts to please and not overwhelm.

Good News For a Change

You know, some evenings I get so depressed watching the TV news, I just get up and shut the thing off and play a game of solitaire. Take tonight for instance. Mailbox bombs, gigantic ammonia leaks in a construction job, escaped prisoners, cop killings — and there were more, but I simply put my mind into the "black-out" position. Isn't there any good news left in the world?

Of course, but good news isn't considered "news" by the media, it seems. For you and me, good news isn't big news — it's the happy things that happen to our friends and neighbors. The new baby's arrival after two week's delay from the ETA is always something that keeps tongues wagging. The granddaughter who gets a coveted place on the honor roll or the young kid down the street who wins a bicycle. The kind of things that colors each of our lives has to be kept in mind or else, by dwelling on the major national and international dilemmas, we will soon lose perspective on life.

In our walk through this world, we need to maintain a balance if we are going to make it. We would be foolish to laugh all the time, and we certainly hope we need not cry all the time. We have to read bad stories, I guess; but it would be nice if there were a measure of pleasant tales to mellow the ugly day's happenings.

I feel the same way about the world of entertainment. I savor the luxury of tossing aside a book I find too risque or violent to read. If the book offends, I can make that decision. The same with violent movies and television shows. Could it be that the public has grown so casual about the ugliness in the world that it does not penetrate our real self? That is really scary.

So having set such a scenario before you, I ask what's the answer? Solomon in all his wisdom wouldn't touch that one, so you aren't going to get much from the likes of me — yet I dare leave you with something to think about.

There have been other times as violent as today, times when more people than now were persecuted and treated unjustly, times when more violent natural disasters took place—and somehow the world survived. Perhaps it is that we get too much news today, too quickly. It becomes overwhelming when one calamity is heaped pell mell onto another before we have a moment to absorb the first. The marvel of instantaneous communication may be too rapid for the mortal mind.

Looking back on some tragedies of earlier times, I think we learned something—not always—but sometimes. We do not realize it, but we may be gaining an insight into what's happening today that will enlighten future generations. Perhaps.

Well, all I promised you was something to think about. I guess I'm still thinking it would be favorable if the networks found just one upbeat story a night to report. I'd thank them if they did.

A Glimpse At The Moon

A few weeks ago, I drove home from the Common Ground Fair just as dark was beginning to wrap the day up and put it to bed. I chose to motor through a Chelsea back road that was open and straight. Above the horizon, the western sky was ablaze with spectacular pinks, purples and blues. I almost ran off the road gazing heavenward.

Along the route, I stopped at the home of friends. After driving into the yard, I turned toward the house and glimpsed at the glowing arc of the moon peeking over a stand of trees in the distance. It was minutes before I knocked at the door. I was transfixed by the giant orb and watched its miraculously swift ascent into the heavens. Even as I watched, I could feel the earth cooling as the warmth of the sun disappeared. It was a scene straight out of Charlie Brown's delightful Halloween story.

For me there is something magic about the moon. I look at it and still find it impossible to believe a human being has been there and walked around in its dust. Little wonder that the Gershwins, Debussy, Schubert and many more composers were impelled to write music about this nocturnal traveler. Ah, well, call me a romantic if you will.

Some years ago, a flight out of Kennedy International Airport was a dozen hours delayed en route to Greece. As a result, we missed connections and spent the night in Brussels, Belgium. My oldest granddaughter was making the trip with me, and we were both pretty exhausted after a sleepless night. I reasoned, however, that neither of us might ever be in that city again, so we quickly exchanged U.S. dollars for Belgium currency and took a nearby train from the airport hotel into the city.

As we came from the train terminal we stepped out onto a vista looking over the entire city. Our eyes were nearly level with a church spire. Again, I was stopped right in my tracks. A sliver of a crescent moon balanced precisely on its upper tip! In my foggy fatigue, I remember little about the city of Brussels, but the memory of that evening picture pasted over it will remain with me forever.

59

The moon seems to have its own brand of brilliance, no matter the country. Once we reached Greece, we welcomed the moon as it shone into our tents anchored beside the Aegean Sea. Its shimmering reflection on that body of water was placid and soothing after miles of trekking up and down hill following a horse and cart. We settled one night in a cemetery near the ancient city of Mycenae, but an overcast sky deprived us the sight of even a small glimpse of the moon.

Several times I was lucky enough to see the moon rise in countries in Central America. Often the lights of the surrounding areas dimmed its luster; but in Belize or Honduras, Mexico or Guatemala, the moon was spectacular.

No matter the country, it's the same moon; and without being obscured by clouds, snow or fog, I expect it packs the same wallop depending on the setting and with whom you share the view. I'd opt for a harvest moon seen through a tangle of trees on a crisp September night in Maine. I am prejudiced, I expect, but the Maine moon has it all over the ones I have seen in other parts of the world.

The Joy of Stamp Collecting

What do you collect? Many of you treasure salt and pepper shakers, cows, sheep, frogs, stamps, coins — well, almost anything that comes in variety and abundance is worthy of assembling to suit your fancy.

This thought came to me the other day when I picked up a colorful brochure at the post office. It was, of course, about stamp collecting. Now that is a great item to collect — as a hobby it is relatively inexpensive, it takes just a little energy to assemble the stamps in glassine pockets and put in books, one learns so much from them, and stamps are always redeemable as a commodity — so they can do nothing but increase in value as the years pass.

My first introduction to collecting stamps was from the late John Mc Cormick — a fine fellow and teacher at the Whitefield school. His wife Catherine or "Kakki," as she was affectionately known by local kids, was the postmaster and John helped out. One day he showed me an impressive array of corner blocks of stamps covering a dozen or more years. I remember thinking, "Wow, he has a great headstart!" As financially strapped as any mother is apt to be, I squirreled away 20¢ now and again to buy four 5¢ stamps in a corner block and tucked them away with some from a former purchase. Gradually, as you know, the cost of a stamp rose from 5 to 10 to 15 to 20¢ to where it is now — 25¢ to send a 1/2 oz. of mail. The 20¢ has grown to $100 for a corner block and my interest in owning a collection of postal stamps has waned; not so my interest in looking at them and enjoying the art they portray.

There are so many series of stamps to collect today. A great series several years ago commemorated the Olympics. Now there are tributes to athletes, cars, scientists, flowers, transportation and even stamp collecting itself. With such little effort, we learn about many things from lapping a stamp and putting it on a letter.

Like winning the sweepstakes, there is another aspect of stamp collecting. Don't overlook the fact you might be handed a double or even a triple printed stamp—or one printed upside down. Each of these mistakes is coveted by collectors. If you come into possession of such a stamp, you may have something of great value. If you were unaware of this fact, you could simply moisten the stamp, affix it to your letter and send it on its way, never realizing what you lost.

To be sure, such an event rarely happens (the postal authorities work hard to assure it doesn't), but there is always that reason to look more closely and speculate!

Another thought: the booklet "The Wonderful World of Stamps" suggests that everyone can get into the act. It says that anyone with an idea for a stamp or suggestion about stamps will be heeded. Simply write your suggestion or design idea to: Citizen's Stamp Advisory Committee, c/o Stamp Information Branch, U.S. Postal Service, Washington, D.C. 20260-6753.

The phamplet ends with this message: "Don't wait another minute to discover the art and fun of stamps. Remember, they not only tell their own story, they also tell about the interesting people who save them."

Introducing stamp collecting to your grandchildren may set the stage for many hours of fun for both of you. Surely it is a far less expensive and less dangerous hobby to enjoy with them than skiing!

The Best Way To Travel

If you're under 30 – oh, shucks, let's say 35 – years of age, you might wonder why us oldsters are so fired up about saving the railroad beds for RAILROADS. Let me tell you.

Plenty of history and more than plenty of memories are locked up in those iron rails for those of us who years ago couldn't hop a plane – and didn't even have a car to drive. If the good old B&A or the Maine Central had not puffed and chugged through the Pine Tree State, lots of us would have "stayed put". We were used to being unable to doing everything we wanted to in those days – especially during war years – but there would have been far fewer memories, for sure.

Here's a run-down of just a few things I remember riding the train. Waiting at the Millinocket depot for Aunt Eva, who could ride from Milo on her husband's pass, was a thrill. The bright headlight as the train rolled its way into the station always made my spine tingle. Aunt Eva seldom kept her appointment with us, but no matter – we saw the train come in!

I would walk to the station in North Whitefield to see the daily Whitefield, Winslow, Wiscasset narrow gauge fume into port. This memory comes through a mist for I was in my pre-teen years when this darling little business lived. But it, too, was love at first sight.

The basketball "specials" that took fans from Millinocket to Bangor to the annual tournament were unavailable to me until I reached 16! The celebrating for a Stearns victory or·a consolation party for a defeat were too notoriously raucous for my mother's taste. Even at 16, I was accompanied!

It is not a happy memory the day I waved goodbye to my husband of one month when his train pulled away from the Bangor siding, taking him to far away places and lands as a Private in the U.S. Engineers. Better the memory when I met him at the Portland station three years later – back from Saipan in the Pacific!

While teaching school in Milo, I took the train to Guilford (a very short ride) to spend Christmas during war years at the farm of Cliff and Bessie

Stone. Cliff met me at the depot in a swirling snow storm with a sleigh and a pair of horses – ah, now that is a beautiful moment to recall. Someday there will be more to tell about this amazing farm couple who adopted stray people like some gather tomatoes. Awesome decisions face you when your lifestyle has taken a dramatic change. My Bernie had passed away after a year's fight with CA. I needed space and time to think about my future, set my sights in line and decide what options to choose to make a rewarding life alone. The railroad proved a solution.

I boarded the train in Brownville Junction one early September evening, determined to travel across the amazing Canadian landscape and "set my ducks in a row," as they say. It was the perfect answer. I was left to my own thoughts. I knew no one on the train. I could step off for an overnight if I wished to see a part of the passing scene. I could stay aboard and speedily complete the journey. What I remember of this adventure was serenity, good food, company to speak with if I wished, sleeping to the clippity-clop of the wheels propelling me to unknown territory. The VIA rail across Canada straightened out my miseries as true as the girders below the Pullman car.

Now do you wonder why I want the trains to come back? They are luxuriously easy to take – you let the engineer do the driving and you, the passenger, ride as a potentate with nothing more strenuous to do than view the fields and urban lands outside. Every child should know the melodies of trains – the whistle tooting, the sizzzz as it slows for a stop, the singing of the wheels and the glorious whirl of wind as you step out onto the platform between cars.

Do I want the trains to come back to Central Maine? You betcha'. If I haven't convinced you, let me know. I'll give you a dozen more reasons to consider.

The Wonder Of Rocks

R ocks. Who could ever be excited about plain, old dirty rocks? I could—and do. I find great joy in seeking out a variegated rock on the beach, recognizing the unexpected design of a rock wall, or passing artfully-placed small boulders in a rock garden. Rocks excite me—and I have found many friends who are equally as (weird, you say?) impressed.

Now I'm talking about everyday finds — unpolished, run-of-the-mill rocks — not tourmalines or amethysts from West Paris or even small nuggets of gold from the Sandy River. Yet I confess I covet those as well.

For instance, I have carried a small, pure black rock picked up by a Maine fisherman on rugged Brimstone Island just off Vinalhaven Island. Beaching a boat on that shore is tricky and not many get there, but the gems you pick up on the beach are as polished and beautiful as if they had been tumbled. Gifts that have kept me amused for at least 20 years.

My dear friend Alice ended her days at the Lincoln County Home in Newcastle. She often walked along the nearby river and pasture land picking up rocks and twigs. She had an uncanny eye for faces, animal shapes and images in these pickings. Often she carried them back to her room and, with a bit of paint and lots of imagination, changed the natural pieces into whimsical curios that were delightful. On my cluttered desk is one that speaks to me of this gentle lady each time I glance its way.

Another friend and I filled our luggage to overflowing with treasures from one of Ireland's gorgeous strands. I don't know how Judy dispersed her gems, but mine might be found in any Irishman's home who showed the least interest in a bit of the ol' sod. I hope St. Patrick and all the other saints (to say nothing of the authorities) will forgive the transgression of taking more than memories from that dear land. Suppose a few stolen rocks matter?

Pure white rocks from Pemaquid, blue-black rocks from Mount Katahdin, pieces of granite from a Hulls Cove quarry, a bit of pink marble broken from a discarded slab—each holds some element of wonder for me. It could easily be determined why—as a lady said to me one day,

"You must have a head full of rocks, Katy, you collect so many." Too close to the truth to be funny!

I stopped at Perhams Gem Store at Trapp Corner the other day. I drooled over the luxurious stones but maintained my cool. Know what single thing I finally bought? No, it was not a rock at all, but a crystal. A bismuth crystal "grown" in Germany. The store manager explained that in Germany a single crystal, in this case bismuth, is heated to a particular degree and the crystals divide and actually grow. It looks like something straight out of "Star Wars" — a myriad of beautiful colors that have emerged in collections of squares, right angles and stars. Indescribable, but beautiful. I paid far more for this than any rock I have picked up, but at $3 it was still a steal.

Today's Trash — Tomorrow's Treasure

A trip to the Maine Museum—or any museum for that matter, may send you home thinking of all the articles you lived with as a child that are today considered antiques.

"Why, we had one of those old crocks in the cellar at home when I was a kid." "Wonder whatever became of that dress form mother used when she did dressmaking?" "My gosh, Dad had an old tool chest in the barn that belonged to his grandfather. It looked a lot better than the one in this display." These are the usual comments you hear at any display—in Maine especially—of tools from another era.

It's true, you know. Every last one of us has thrown things away we wish we had saved. The mundane articles around any house get taken for granted just as people do when they become part of our daily routine. Perhaps now is the time to stop and rethink what has value and what does not. As fast as things change today and new, better, more advanced articles come along to replace the old ones, the harder it is to see the merit in "saving". Perhaps there are a couple of reasons for that.

First of all, with the increased affluence of today's economy, things are easier to acquire. We don't have to save, make do—or more importantly, MAKE the things we need for any task. "Easy come, easy go" is an apt phrase more true today than ever before. There is no reason to give special attention to "things" because they are easily replaced.

Then there is the issue of storage. Condominiums and compact modular homes are built to have a place for everything (and everything MUST be in its place), but there's little extra space for storage. No longer the giant garrets or barn lofts where a complete household of furniture could be put away without a bit of trouble. Moving into tight, compact living quarters has certainly divested us of places to keep tomorrow's antiques.

All the more reason today to look over our own acquisitions, and spend some time assuring they will not be relegated to the garbage in the next generation. Let's think about that for a bit.

If you are fortunate enough to have a signed painting or piece of furniture, almost certainly someone else will be interested in it. What you do is—somewhere on it or in it—write where you acquired it, who had it before you did and how you got it. A future family member will thank you for so doing. It also will bring greater value to the object.

For insurance purposes, it is advisable to have a photo of the object. This is equally important if the object is stolen. With a photograph it can be correctly identified. Even a B&W photo you take yourself will almost certainly suffice as identification.

This probably sounds as if I think you have a Winthrop desk or a set of Hitchcock chairs or an early Church landscape. Not at all. Sometimes the sentimental value of the family object is as valuable as the monetary value. My daughter-in-law gives a place of prominent honor to a plated silver candlestick that belonged to her husband's grandmother. Because this object spans four generations, counting her children, it weaves a link with family and is thus a sentimental treasure. So it must be with things in your home.

Caution is the word. Think carefully before you clear the house of potential treasures during the next cleaning urge. Remember the early comics printed on newspaper you read as a young person? Wonder what those coveted pages are worth today? Well, you wouldn't believe it. The law of supply and demand works all the time. The scarcer the commodity, the more people will pay to own it. And it doesn't have to be a 1928 Maxwell even. (Wow, wouldn't it be glorious to own one of those jobs?) Remember, today's trash just could be tomorrow's treasure. Even rag pickers and junk dealers make money. Think about it.

An Insatiable Appetite For Books

I came late to the love of books. As a child I scorned the leaves covered with words. There were few books in my home and that might be part of the reason. I was unfamiliar with them. Even in college, I read what I had to, but confess to a lot of scanning. It was probably when the long winter days and nights kept me house-bound with my children that the real treasure residing in a book seeped into my consciousness. At any rate, today I have an insatiable appetite for all things printed.

A bookstore is my undoing—the temptation to throw the well-calculated budget out of whack is overwhelming. I remember a small book store/coffee shop in Dingle, Ireland. I was working on the final dollars allotted to "mad money" when I found this gem. Irish writers—whose wit is not ever to be topped—beckoned from every shelf. Forget the coffee, even the aromatic Irish bread. I bogged myself down with the tomes. I couldn't count the number of times I have reread the books from that delightful shop. Even more frequently than reading them I have goaded others to read and know the pleasure of Irish writers.

Locally, a book sale at Hubbard Free Library in Hallowell, Lithgow Library in Augusta or Gardiner Public Library in Tilbury Town finds me early at the doors. It is surprising, too, how many people are bookworms. Book lovers are as prone to elbow jabbing and reaching in front of each other as shoppers at the after-Christmas mall sale. There is a more positive side of this story, methinks. Pleasure from the book purchases will last far longer than the mall buys.

There is a most delightful children's book store in Gardiner that should be well-known to parents and grandparents. Tree-House Book Shop and Gallery is right on Gardiner's Brunswick Avenue with vivacious Maggie Smith running the show. Maggie has an uncanny sense about what children should be exposed to in book fare. She tries to read every book she presents so she can suggest for the proper age—and tell something of the story. Don't think for a minute that selecting a child's book is child's play (excuse the pun). Finding calm, pleasant stories that portray virtues we hope will be instilled in children, and all tastefully illustrated is no small chore. Maggie grasps the importance of literary efforts and carries some real "finds" other places do not offer.

Every Friday morning Protectors of Animal Life Society (PALS) volunteers are at the Turnpike Mall unpacking books, magazines and puzzles as early as 8 a.m. The ladies assure you that books you might be looking for are quite apt to be stored with others back at their homes and you have only to ask. They'll do the research and come back the following week with your item. It's altogether too easy to lose your sense of time and tasks as you look through their wares.

In Hallowell, Leon Tibbetts has managed a used book store for years. It amazes me the lengths to which he will go to locate an out-of-print or unknown author for the customer. Dealers know of his efforts, but others should know of his service.

Bunkhouse Books on the Lewiston Road just out of Gardiner performs a similar service and has a rare collection of Maine authors — perhaps their speciality.

The Book Boob, a title I quite often give myself, quickly learns where to scrounge for treasures in their community. If you happen to be of this ilk, I feel you should know some of the places to begin your book searching. Careful, though, your purchases will quickly necessitate new book shelves in your home.

One of the poorest things about Belize, where I lived for two years, was the lack of reading material. The Peace Corps Center had an adequate library, but the main library in the country had few new books. The stacks were filled with very soiled, dog-eared copies of rather old, outdated books. Few bright enticing book covers to impel people to look to reading as an adventure. Pity!

Elbert Hubbard captured the essence of books. In **The Philistine** he wrote, "This will never be a civilized country until we expend more money for books than we do for chewing gum." 'Nuff said.

A Product of the Depression

The Depression of the early 30s did strange things to kids. Even children not deprived sensed the need to look to tomorrow and save. I don't know if the bank failure was what the sages had in mind when they cautioned "save for a rainy day," but I do know that era left an indelible mark on me.

Paper bags are a case in point. I harbor an absolute fetish about those useful grocery-luggers. I fold them carefully, often better than my wearing apparel, and place them next to dozens of their kin squirreled away from past shopping sprees. When the accumulation gets overwhelming, they are taken to a larger storage place. After several months of this idiocy, off to the food co-op or the thrift shop they go. I feel quite virtuous about this scenario. A carry-over from past days, you see.

The same saving grace (?) goes for twine, string, elastic bands and paper clips — I adore paper clips. Then there is garbage, or in more lady-like terms, table scraps. It seems quite horrible to simply grind up peelings, pulps and rinds, compact them into a neat square and cart them off (or rather PAY to have them carted off) to the local land-fill. There they will be relegated to nothingness. How much better to trot them out to the back of the house, dig a hole, sprinkle all this natural waste into the hole and cover it! Back in the soil where it originated, it will return to nature and do something to enrich the soil — even if nothing is ever planted there again. Although I do not recommend this practice, I have been known to take ALL kitchen refuse to such an extreme. I perhaps had the only garden in Maine where ham and chicken bones turned up now and then. Needless to say, there were no household pets in the family.

If the 30s were your formative years, you undoubtedly have a cellar stocked with jams, pickles and other canned things — against hard times. We also kept jugs of water — refreshed every six months, a battery-operated radio, a flashlight and spare batteries nearby. Everything ready in case of an emergency, you know.

71

Having reached those coveted years of retirement, we may well laugh at such quirks. But we have endured—and learned much about "making do". We are in a better position to cope with scarcities predicted for the future. It may take more than a hairpin to hold back the ravages of an economy gone bonkers, or more than a hand in the dike (no finger would ever be considered, even in Holland) to stem the flow of the appalling cost of food and clothing; but I'll wager a molasses cookie that folks over 55 manage a sight better than those 25. Experience in COPING may be one of the best things that has happened to older people since Social Security.

Grocery Shopping — Then and Now

There was a time when not too long ago that a week's groceries might use up most of the five dollar bill you had tucked away in your pocket. No more. Those days are long gone, but they remain a warm memory — and not just because of the cost of things.

The store was usually a corner market where the man behind the counter was a produce clipper, meat cutter, local newsman, bagger, wrapper, calculator and a good neighbor. This friendly gent with his blood-smeared white apron walked around the store and gathered your items, one at a time as you called them out. He could give you a prime cut of beef, weight out a chicken, pump a quart of molasses or a gallon of kerosene, and still have time and energy enough to suggest a piece of penny candy for the small fry you had in tow or suggest a new way to do a pot roast. His was usually a one-man operation — until his son got into the business too.

When you seemed to come to the end of your list, he had suggestions. "How about some nice fresh-dug potatoes? Just got a delivery from Masardis this morning. Some great early apples, too. Green — just right for a pie! That's all? OK."

With this, he would (in summer) push his straw hat off his forehead, take a stubby pencil out of his shirt pocket and grab a USED BAG from under the counter. Item by item he would list the price, then add them up. No calculator or cash register that counts — nothing but his agile brain. The bill might look something like this:

pork chops	.32
bananas	.18
bread	.09
milk	.16
kerosene	.17

After listing, he checked off each item again with the point of his pencil. Once this was completed, he would sing out the answer and turn the paper around for you to see.

If you asked to pay by check other patrons would surely have looked to see who had money enough to own a checking account! If you did not pay cash, you would ask if the purchase could be "set down". This meant that father or mother would be in on payday to "settle up".

This comparison with shopping I did back in the 30s struck me the other day as I left the local supermarket. I gathered all the things I wanted. I chose pre-packaged meat, vegetables, fruits and peanuts. I saw more things than I wanted or needed and spent far more than I had planned to spend. I wheeled my cart up to the checkout; and although the clerks are polite and gracious, they don't know anything about local happenings — they may even live in a far away town.

As I got in the car, I looked at the sales slip. Date, time, cash register number, cashier's name, items purchased, cost per item, total cost — minus coupons if any — the denomination of currency I presented and the amount of change I would receive. All this ending with the inane statement "Have a Good Day!" The sales tab is an unbelievable array of everything you ever would want to know about what you bought and where your money goes. I bought five food items — no meat — and two paper products. The bill was over ten dollars. Little to eat even at that.

Another variance is that, in most cases, young boys no longer carry your bags to the car. Likely as not it is some agile senior citizen who hoists your purchases into the open car door. They always have a pleasant smile for you.

I guess some of the changes could be described as better. But you know, I kinda' liked it when there was the usual storekeeper to chew the fat with a little, to swap some homespun yarns with. Somehow it doesn't seem quite right that we don't have more time to combine business with pleasure as we go through the demands of the day.

Treasure Amid the Rubble

Rummaging, my mother used to call it. Definition: Pawing through a pile of trash or treasures from another era. Perhaps that's what we do at a rummage sale. Mother instilled in me that urge I always get when confronted by such an accumulation. Rummaging, more often than not, is worth the effort.

I'd like to explain a few cases. Mother spent many of her final years living in Milo. She was a woman that stayed a stranger only a short time. People gravitated to her as they do to a pretty flower. She was, indeed, a beautiful woman. On more than one occasion she was on hand when a friend's attic was under attack. There is a stunning oil painting of a barn and farm yard on my walls from one forage. Mother told the story.

"Effie, this is an interesting painting I found behind that box of rags. Who painted it, do you know?" mother asked.

"Phew, that old thing has been around ever since I lived here. Guess it belonged to George's mother. Throw it out the window onto the truck parked below. I don't want it."

Mother admitted she stopped and gave it another scrutiny. It was intact, not a rip—perhaps more than a little dusty, but she saw it as something worth saving. So inquired:

"Effie, you don't really want to toss this away, do you? I think it is quite nice."

"Look, Bessie, I've come up here to clean out and clean out is what I want to do. If you want to cart that old thing home, go to it," was the answer.

Mother admitted she protested just long enough to show sincerity, and did "tote" the piece home in her old '41 Chevy coupe. My husband framed the work in an old barn board frame, we carefully dusted and cleaned it, and it is considered quite a treasure by my family. The story is nearly as fascinating as the art work.

Mother did have an eye for beauty. At another time she found a large tin disk painted with an ad for pipe tobacco. It looks about the size of the round sled kids use to scale down snowy hills today. Mom may have paid a quarter or so for this item and took it to a talented young man, George Hamlin, who was doing some fine Pennsylvania Dutch decor at the time. It, too, now graces my parlor wall. Sometimes I gaze at it and wonder about the painting underneath. I saw a similar disk in a shop one day with the original ad still intact. It carried a price tag of several hundred dollars! I like my Dutch wedding scene worth at least that much.

So, you see, I naturally come by the passion to find a thing of unusual beauty among clutter. I love to go into Ginny Diplock's crammed little shop in Hallowell for just that reason. There is something different every day. Now Cathy Waller has taken the adjoining shop and is showing fascinating fashions from another era. Those two shops work like giant magnets on me. I stop in to "look" even when I don't have the time. I think you would be just as impressed as I am with the two little wooden characters I found there once. They were created by an amateur artist of the 20s or 30s. Not great works of art, surely, but delightful expressions of one person's talent.

I feel sorry for those who turn up their noses at rummaging. I have spent considerable time in metal junkyards scrounging for old pieces of iron. The make interesting pieces to place among the flowers of my aspiring garden.

Perhaps it's the Yankee Trader in me, but finding a treasure amid the rubble is as exciting for me as winning the sweepstakes. The odds are better, too.

Pre-TV Amusements From My Childhood

Do youngsters today wonder what kids their age did before television? Lately I've spent considerable time myself, trying to remember what we did during those days of the 20s and 30s. As unexciting as the activities were then, we did have fun!

There were lots of shenanigans, of course. One kid daring another to climb trees, jump over fences, steal apples in season and be general nuisances to the folks in the neighborhood—yet I don't ever recall being so unruly that the group was labeled a "gang" or was ostracized. We were competitive, and really quite creative in the games we played.

Of a certainty hop-scotch, jump rope and marbles were as popular then as now. Perhaps playing such games were more consistent and never were the accoutrements of games purchased. We cut a piece of old clothesline for the jump rope (some children today hardly know that clothes were ever hung on a clothes line to dry—tsk!), we made hop scotch grids by taking a stick and drawing it on a piece of open ground—or if we were fortunate enough to be near a paved (and thus smooth) piece of land, we used chalk from our own small blackboards—and when store-bought marbles were not available, we resorted to a collection of round pebbles. This last, not a very successful substitute; but we made do.

A favorite game was CADDY. Perhaps others played a variation of the game and called it by another name. It involved a clothespin whittled to a point, a flat stick (we just went to the wood shed and picked up a piece of kindling), and the front steps. The idea was to whack that clothespin as far from the steps as possible because the opponent had to pick it up and throw it back trying for all they were worth to hit the bat stick. How we scored and all the intricacies of the game are gone form my memory, but it filled many evening hours for a bunch of us who lived on Pine Street.

During summer days I recall many hours with a friend, Ellie Morrison, writing a newspaper. We called it the **Daily Buzz** and filled it with unparalleled trivia about people we knew. Everything—from the Chief of

Police carrying out a very obese girl in our class down a ladder during a fire to a fabricated love affair between a spinster school teacher and a local vagabond—spiced the pages of our chronicle. Thank heaven no one got to read our literary efforts except family—and they had to pay a penny or two to do even that. When I think back on those churned up columns, they do not seem any more ridiculous than Saturday Night Live episodes. Could it be we were ahead of our time?

Play-acting was big in my life. Ellie and I took countless ocean cruises from the ramp leading into a nearby cinema. We were imaginative, providing ourselves with diversions somewhat similar to what TV is offering today. I suspect that using our inherent creativity was more satisfying than TV is, but who knows?

Babies spent hours banging a wooden spoon against a pie pan or catching feathers that might be left over from a Sunday chicken. Even if toys had been available to buy, there was never money enough for necessities—let alone toys!

Perhaps not one of us would elect to go back to those days; but they were not really dull, nor uninteresting, nor did we feel deprived. Every one of us was in the same boat, and we knew nothing about that Jones family we try to keep up with today. I don't think I would have wanted to.

Are We Victims of Advertising and Sales?

When the snow swirls about the door and the temperature sends a chill down the spine, stove dealers are out in force. What better compensates for a cold wintry day than a fire crackling in the old kitchen stove (do you remember those?) or the fireplace. It's "cozy" we want, a picture book scene of how life was when we perhaps had more control over our own existence. I know, there are many who wouldn't trade those days for the luxurious life of today no matter how they dream about a warm fire to snuggle up to.

But as much as I would like to emphasize the merit in providing your own source of heat or food or entertainment, that's not the point of this piece. The subject is how well the tradesman uses events of the day to tempt us into his emporium. It rains and the umbrella salesman pushes his wares to the front of the store. Snow is predicted so the shovels get top billing in the daily news. Manufacturers of "coolers" have a great time pressing their drink during the heat of summer. Now it's hot-mulled cider time, and at every part of the market there are the ingredients to mull your own. The promoters are doing everything right when they follow this procedure. They also know just how impressionable we are! I find it a real challenge to short circuit their intent, don't you?

If the latest commercial has suggested I will be guilty of ring-around-the-collar if I don't use a certain detergent, I go out of my way to bypass their product. If a pain reliever promoter vows I will never get over that tired, achy feeling so quickly as when I buy their pain killer, I grit my teeth, almost always determine all I need is a good night's sleep and buy nothing. Usually it works. I resist being brainwashed into believing a little pain is unbearable. It also turns me completely off to be treated like a complete ignoramus by TV commercials. They can't make me believe that people acting like idiots to promote a super fiber-packed cereal reaches an intelligent adult. Perhaps they don't think too many of us are intelligent!

Truly, I am not as ornery as I sound. I have pretty frugal ideas about purchases, as my friends will attest. I try to provide myself with the necessities and let it go at that. Two years away from the freedom to buy anything taught me as they say in **Lake Wobegone Days**, "If you can't find it you probably can get along without it." My conviction is that too many times we are wooed, coaxed or unduly urged to part with our money before we reflect long enough on the departure. That might be one of the reasons why family dollars keep running out before the next paycheck arrives.

It probably has always been this way. A friend, in a moment of agitation, told me the other day, "We teach students all about history and geography today, but don't spend any time at all training people how to live or how to make hard choices in this society." It could do nothing but help if some time in school were spent dealing with consumer ideals — only, of course, if overworked teachers had one more minute to teach yet another discipline. Could it be that homes should pick up the slack?

Phone Philosophies

When I went to call on my son's family in their new country home, I was surprised to find his youngest daughter involved in a lengthy telephone conversation. I wondered, "Who can she be talking to on the phone? It was just connected two hours ago and she certainly has not been in this town long enough to make friends already." I should have known the answer. Young people today see the telephone as an instrument to use — like a can opener or hair dryer. They think nothing of calling a friend across the street — or across the country!

Driving home I tried to analyze the event as a young person would — not easy since I was young several decades ago. There are no dollar signs before their eyes as they dial a number — in fact, perhaps no one has ever told them it COSTS MONEY! Balancing their cavalier (my opinion) use of the phone with that of my upbringing is a fine act. In my day we didn't see it as a way to "reach out and touch someone" — it was for use in emergencies: when the house caught on fire, when a child was sick and needed a doctor, or when someone couldn't get home because of a blizzard. Sitting in the middle between my mother's horror in running up a phone bill and a granddaughter who never gives it a thought, does provide food for thought.

Perhaps in her entire life Mom never made more than a dozen out-of-state calls. She had good reason to, and the following story surely will convince you that she should have.

Mother was one of the youngest of 12 children. Her brothers and sisters had moved away from home and from Maine long before she grew up. She still missed each one of them. One brother in particular had gone to West Virginia, met a lady there and married her, and had returned home only once in 50 years — and that was for the funeral of their parents. Mother's lifelong wish was to go to West Virginia to visit Jim and his family.

It happened Mother was living with my family about the time a small insurance matured and she felt pretty "rich" with the unexpected check in

81

hand. "Mom," I said, "why not call Jim and his family and see how they are? Perhaps, if it is convenient for them, you might even think about taking a trip south and visiting them," I suggested. The idea was alien to her — she would never have initiated such an adventure on her own. It took me no time at all to have directory assistance get the W. Virginia number and put the call through. I left her to her conversation but was surprised to hear a sob shortly thereafter. The awesome truth was that Jim, his wife said, had passed away a month before; and because the family had been apart for so long, there seemed little need of informing the relatives up north.

It was weeks before Mom began to realize there was no further need to plan a trip to the coal mining district of the Virginias. Her recurring lamentation was, "Why didn't I call sooner?"

I am coming around to my granddaughter Kris' way of thinking. If you miss your friends back home, call them and tell them. Tomorrow may be too late. Even so, I must admit, I never dial a long distance number without the vision of the month's phone bill before my eyes. It's simply a conditioned (and still necessary) response from so many years of counting pennies, without bringing into the focus the amazing bang we get for our buck when the telephone company connects us with a long time friend or business associate. I just hope I am not already too old to learn some of the wisdom of a sharp young granddaughter.

Doing Laundry in the Good Old Days

I saw the book so long ago that I can't even remember its name — a book containing dramatic pictures of clotheslines snapped throughout the entire United States. Such trivial portrayals, yet surely a facet of life we no longer see. Clothesline memories stirred in my psyche with each page I turned. All thoughts of the days when we pulled fabric between the ringers of the wash and hung it to dry are not unpleasant, yet are well-imprinted on a mother's historic score.

It was mid-January (for openers), deep in rural Maine. I was fortunate to have an electric washing machine that churned clothes automatically, but all other chores relating to the Monday wash were manually performed. Once they were rinsed, wrung and shaken, hanging the clothes was the hard part. Next I put on boots, hat, coat — and if available — roomy gloves. The short step to the wind-blown front of the house was horrible! My mother called it a "step-mother's breath". It was alarmingly cold; and even as the steam rose from the basketed laundry, the top garment froze into an immovable object before it reached the clothesline. Those were the days, too, when every diaper was handled a dozen times from the time it left the infant's body, through the wash routine, to folding, to the time it returned to protect the baby's bottom.

As unpleasant as the hanging-out was, taking clothes from the line was even worse. Connect wet fabric with a zero-degree length of line and the adherence is unbelievable. In seconds, exposed fingers (for one needed every bit of dexterity possible) became numb — and unwilling to operate at all. Sheer determination kept me at the task. Once a diaper (for instance) was removed, I had to bend it to make it collapse enough to be put in the basket. Duplicate this operation a few dozen times with snowy winds whipping about, trying to keep an ear and an eye on what three young lads might be up to back in the cozy kitchen, and you'll understand why women are referred to as the "stronger" sex. Survival of the species depended on such strength. And the job wasn't yet completed. I carried a basket overloaded with sheets of rigid cloth into the house — using an icy derriere to close the door behind me. Then, one by one, I looked for places to drape the frozen clothes. Over the radiator, on the bathroom door, over the wooden clothes rack, behind the heavenly wood stove in the kitchen. Gradually the whole process was finished. After a half an hour I found the mop and began wiping up under the frozen, dripping items.

Why in the name of all that is important and necessary in life, did people put themselves through this regimen? Don't ask me. It was the way I was brought up—I did what hundreds of other mothers were doing—who was I to take the easy way out? I conformed, as I bet you did if you lived before the era of the automatic washer/dryer. Besides, wasn't this the way to build character—and strength?

Then there were the glorious days of spring when I couldn't wait to finish the wash so I could step into the sunshine, with the boys safely underfoot, and hang the wash accompanied by a warming breeze. Quickly forgotten were the awesome days of before. I rejoiced for such a satisfying task, and the luxury of sitting on the steps with a breathtaking view of the Sheepscot Valley. The boys and I took time to read as we savored the coming of a new growing season.

Young mothers must be amazed by the recounting of this episode. I look back and marvel myself. I also marvel that I could live to tell about it and be glad, honestly glad, to have lived at such a time. A time when perhaps I had more control than I believed I did. Life forty years ago was hard, but I'm not so sure it wasn't easier in many ways—we did have time for cloistered family. We spent a great deal more time together—not always happy time—but we got along fine.

Weren't the early people wise to decide that Monday — only one day a week — was enough to do the family laundry?

The Value of Corn

Since I can remember, popcorn has been a family ritual. As a child I often had a 5-cent bag of it when I went to the Saturday matinee at the Millinocket Opera House (what a decadent use of the word opera), but it was not until I married one of the Perry boys that I learned just how special popcorn could be.

Snacks were few during the Depression. Little wonder parents got a greater (forgive the expression) "bang" for their money buying corn, putting it over the fire and letting it pop. Most of the kids of that era got hooked on the munchie, an addiction they carried through life.

Ours was a big, old two-and-a-half story house in Whitefield that was heated by a wood furnace. On a cold winter night, Bernie would stand by the kitchen sink, fill the wire popper with just the right measure of corn and head for the cellar. The embers, from day-long burning, would be just right at that time. In just a minute or two he would come back to the kitchen toting a snowy mound of fluffy corn that continued its sporadic popping on the way.

A special, large wooden bowl we had bought for a couple of bucks at an auction accommodated the corn perfectly. A bit of salt and a swirl of golden butter from a tin cup he had thoughtfully set on the back of the kitchen range was all the flavoring our modest treat needed.

The number of hands that dipped into that bowl increased over the years until there were six pairs reaching for the stuff. We often washed the popcorn down with hot chocolate in winter and fruit juice during the warmer times of year, but no matter the season we enjoyed popcorn on a regular basis.

The habits of youth have remained. A visit to the homes of any of my sons and their families invariably ends with a bowl of popcorn. Alas! Another generation of kids have become popcorn poppers. I kinda' like the idea.

Corn is such a wondrous commodity. It is to most Latin countries what rice is to the Orient – the basic food. I remember vendors along the streets in Peru steaming ears of corn and urging people to buy. Wrapped in their insulating husks, the ears seemed too water-logged for my taste; and besides, the threat of contaminated water deterred a purchase, but it was tempting.

Botanically speaking, corn is a unique, giant grass and has, so the encyclopedia says, only one close relative. Perhaps no other crop adapts itself to different soils and climates as well. It was discovered and developed in the New World, spread to the Mediterranean and then to other parts of the world. It is as valuable as a money crop as it is for food.

There are corn fritters, corn muffins, corn chowder, corn pudding, corn pone, cornstarch (for puddings and thickening), corn balls (that should be available not only at Christmas) and corn "gems" — what variety, what delicious smells and tastes the mere mention of some things made from corn evokes.

What began as a thought about popcorn has turned into a hymn in celebration of maize — not wholly inappropriate. It may be a bit corny, but how about three cheers for popcorn? Ready? And one, two, HURRAH! HURRAH! HURRAH!

The Maine State Museum - An Inexpensive Outing

A re you looking for inexpensive fun? Have I got news for you. Think about the Maine State Museum. It's a fantastic way to enjoy a winter afternoon—the kids will be stimulated to ask questions, and parents will have to keep on their toes to find answers. If you haven't been convinced yet that Maine is a terrific place to live, a visit to the Museum will do the trick.

One Sunday, a small notice in the paper indicated that Don Bassett, the Museum's graphic designer, would talk about all the things you need to know to display museum (or your own) treasures tastefully, effectively and with proper lighting. Only 25 people could be accommodated in the small conference room—and the limit had been reached. It was fantastic to learn all the problems one must overcome to stage a long-term exhibit, such as the beautiful Maine gem collection. Don took us step-by-step, pointing out how many times what he thought was right turned out to be wrong. Time and again he looked for material or fabrics to achieve the effect he wanted. Strange, but after much persistence the right things almost leaped out at him—in the most unexpected places. Along with gaining the right ambience for the display, great concern is given to use of materials that will emit no toxic fumes or gases, or will in any way damage the items on display.

Once the hour-long exhibit was over, I dashed downstairs and raced to the gem exhibit. I had seen it before, but looked at it this time in a wholly different way. I knew the problems, I had heard of the solutions that took months to find, and saw with amazement just how what Don had hoped to do was done. Surely he is a crackerjack in his field of design.

Don is only one of the extremely effective staff people at the Museum. I hesitate to name any for fear of overlooking another; but several with whom I have worked over the years (in a very minor way, I confess) could easily be toasted with the best of any in the country in a comparable position.

A loyal group of volunteers keeps the museum staffed. On the way home I met Barbara Patterson at the reception desk. She was busy counting visitors as they came in.

"Barbara," I asked, "Do you have many people visit the museum on a Sunday afternoon?"

"We certainly do, Katy. We are open from 1 p.m. until 4. Almost every weekend over 1,000 people visit. This is during the winter. As the season warms up, the number will increase. I think the state gets the best bang for its buck right here. Maine people and visitors come through here and I hear them talking about how impressed they are with the exhibits."

Certainly that is an unsolicited endorsement from one who should know. Barbara has worked at the desk there for more than a few years.

Right now the entrance to the Cultural Building is under construction; and it is a little difficult—not at all impossible, just slightly inconvenient—to visit, but you should. There are many lifelike displays and more are coming soon. For the remainder of the winter there will be special lectures every two weeks (on Sunday afternoon) and you can learn more about them by watching the papers or by calling the Museum during the week.

"The Museum is only closed four days a year," Barbara said. "It doesn't cost anything to see three floors of exhibits; and with a lecture thrown in every once in a while, I don't know where you'd get a better bargain," she added. Isn't that what I told you in the beginning?

The Power of the Mind

I awakened the other morning and looked at the bedside clock. Five minutes before six. FIVE MINUTES BEFORE SIX! Yipes, I was being picked up at 6 to drive to a Boston meeting with a friend. Breathlessly, I jumped out of bed and ran to the bathroom, only to stop dead in my tracks when reality dawned. This was Monday — the trip south was to be on Tuesday. I collapsed into a nearby chair and tried to calm my unnecessary apprehension.

Just this morning before I woke up, I saw myself at a lawn party which included President Reagan. Fancy that. To further complicate matters, my frivolity with the politicians made me forget to pick up my daughter-in-law, who had plans to spend the night with me. This oversight dawned on me as I brushed my teeth with the President's toothbrush — complete with Presidential seal. Please don't think I am deranged. There is absolutely no accounting for what a relaxed mind can do. This brings me to the issue.

The Public Broadcasting System has been carrying a series of programs relating to the mind, which I have believed for years is one of the last unexplored regions of this world. I have followed the programs haphazardly, but enough to have my belief reinforced. We, if we knew how, could cure many of our ills and make our lives less traumatic. First of all, as with so many things, we must have faith that such a thing is possible. Are you skeptical?

Think, then, about the placebo — that innocent little sugar-coated pill that the subject believes is medication. By believing one will be eased of whatever ailment one is experiencing, one is cured. The silly pill certainly has not done it. One has mentally helped oneself. During a recent study, scientists have positively shown that through mental concentration, serious ailments can be cured or alleviated. This is not hokum — it is scientific research that indicates we DO have great charge over our own well being. The impediment to this theory is a negative attitude. Then it is impossible for such a situation to be successful. We deny ourselves full use of that marvelous part of our body — our mind.

It was many years ago that Norman Vincent Peale brought his book **The Power of Positive Thinking** to the public. It was so long ago that many younger people have not been exposed to this logical thinking. Thinking positively — far better than thinking negatively — does make for a more complacent, happy and productive person. Of course, N.V.P. said it far more eloquently; but don't take my word for it — get the book at your local library and find out for yourself how well he states his theory.

Several years ago, I worked with Eve Weir and Nancy Pulsifer, both declared psychics and members of the quartet called "The Harpswell Sound". Eve wrote a small book on reality which she called **Pocket Book of Change** — lots of connotations embedded in that title alone. One line of this fascinating little lesson tells us, "Life force is at your command constantly." Let it be said that Eve Weir wrote the book in 1972 — long before ''E.T.'' hit the scene — but the message is the same. This is followed by another chapter that tells us, "You can change your thought habits." both Peale and Weir teach and encourage each of us to guide our lives by the best use of our mind — that under-utilized part of our being.

So many years ago Virgil wrote in the Aeneid, "Mens agitat molem" — translation: "Mind moves matter." The idea has been around a long time. Why are we just now beginning to explore it?

A Yen For Bread

There's no accounting for why some moods strike. I rarely read cookbooks, yet last week I had a genuine yen to bake bread. It has been years — well, about three — since I really got into the dough dish. I was looking for something zingy — like garlic bread — nothing sweet or dessert-like. I didn't want biscuits or muffins — just yeast bread that I could jazz up. It was not easy — it lead me to scan the half dozen cookbooks I have gathered over the years.

One, a **Maine Rebekahs Cook Book**, 1939, was my first choice. A small penciled note in my mother's handwriting said, "This book was given to me by David Reed, 1945." Well, the nostalgia trip began right there. Mother had helped to take care of infant David when his parents brought him home from the Bangor Hospital. We were neighbors, and the Reeds were exceptionally good friends with our family. In fact, I used their piano to practice on as a teenager. Can you imagine greater love than two music lovers voluntarily submitting to such torture?

The first page of the book identified past presidents of the Rebekahs in Maine. Each name was followed by the years of service and a chosen motto. I read them all. I found that of Martha E. Libby, who served as president from 1938 to 1939, especially pleasing. "To give is to live. We're only a part of the rest of us." Thought provoking, isn't it? As well as the Rebekahs turned out their book, it didn't fill my need that day, so I turned to another.

This was a clothbound book (each specially made, I wondered?) done by some group of women in Southern Maine — it was in no way identified. The clue to the origin was small historic anecdotes at the end of the pages, such as, "The Simpson Road in Saco was laid out in 1798 and named after Benjamin Simpson who participated in the Boston Tea Party." This was under a recipe for Sun-Gold Potato Mold. The fascinating thing about this book is that the pages are all handwritten or hand-lettered. Gives it great personality and makes you wonder what the writer looked like, how she lived and what her kitchen smelled like! I treasure this book. It had once been owned and used by the late Eleanor Emerson of Pittston and her devoted friend and companion, Helena Joy of Gardiner. A run-through of all the bread recipes – including oatmeal, white yeast, potato, orange, Irish and the like – did not tempt me. I closed the cover and went on to the next one.

The **Millinocket Cook Book**, compiled by the Women's Fellowship of the First Congregational Church of Millinocket, was done in 1950. Over the years, this gift from a fellow teacher, Helen Russell, is so marred with splashings from earlier baking many pages are unreadable. It has some great ideas and is charmingly illustrated by the late Mrs. Robert Hume. I began this search, remember, for bread; but I got so caught up in memories of family favorites from another era, that the morning turned into afternoon before I realized. Strange how the most used part of the book was the cakes and cookies section. This certainly would indicate the desire to please little boys, wouldn't it?

As the afternoon waned, I finally determined to do the shredded wheat bread that mother had so often made for Dr. and Mrs. Richard Stubbs in their State Street, Augusta home. As it sat to "rise," the aroma of yeast and molasses filled the house. I felt virtuous in the ability to create such an aroma.

Alas, the aroma was the best part of the effort. I have always known that baking bread, like painting or making pots, demands constancy. My three-year lapse in baking was all too evident. If you noticed birds around Middle Street in Hallowell having a hard time getting airborne, it's quite possible they were lunching at my bird feeder. Heavy stuff!

Tea Talk

There is a small, rambling white house cuddled halfway up a Hallowell hill where friends gather every day to discuss world situations. The subjects are as different as those who assemble. It may well be 1989's version of the pot-bellied stove in country stores.

There seem to be no set rules for becoming a member of this elite group, simply a yen for a slow wind-down to the day's work, a moment to savor a cuppa' coffee or tea and the joy of sharing time with people of similar tastes but dissimilar opinions. And that, my friends, is where the color of the sessions takes on a vibrant hue.

Not being the hostess of such a community, I am reluctant to do more than synopsize the personalities. Let's say most are professional ladies — all bent on dedication to community affairs, having a strong tendency to involve themselves with organizations that benefit their families and their city. They are a caring, constructive and determined lot. Each brings a view of subjects based on years of living (perhaps in a neighboring state or even a foreign land), differing political and religious persuasions, financial base and education. What all of them possess, however — and most important, is tolerance. The discussions are often heated with extremely divergent viewpoints expressed; yet the parting is always friendly, without rancor or hostility.

Rarely do you feel any opinions have been changed as a result of the hour or so spent in that efficient kitchen. But there has almost certainly been an opportunity to see the subject from a 360 degree plane. One has to go away seeing their firm judgment in a far wider perspective. It boils down to a civilized discussion and, as a result, a learning experience. I often wonder how far-reaching into families and the community are the results of those afternoon gatherings.

Often children from seven-year-olds to high school students join in for a soft drink and a "listen". The model kids do that. They just listen. Rarely do they offer a comment — unless, of course, a subject is broached that they feel has an impact on them. Then THEY are heard. Nice arrangement.

I came home one recent afternoon, really trying to analyze this unique daily event. It was immediately apparent, I thought, that the homeowners are offering a needed service. I live alone and need some spirited communication with others. One lady's husband spends days away from home on business – she also savors the time with her contemporaries. Another needs this transition between a fast-paced business day and beginning dinner. Yet another enjoys time to catch up with old friends when she returns to visit. Now and then, a gentleman comes aboard. Fact is, HE has some difficulty being heard – but his offerings are always well received.

Then there is the family pooch, always on the look-out for a morsel – the pet provides a wisp of beastly balance to the day. A valuable contribution.

It would not surprise me a bit if the discussions around that well-scrubbed oak kitchen table are not as apt and important as those Ben Johnson recounted in his writings.

Speaking of the English bard, Johnson – whose name I have always spelled wrongly – I call on him to put the cap on this piece from his "Every Man In His Humor": "I do honor the very flea of his dog." That's just about the way the Central Street "Gang of 8-10" might sum up their sessions.

The Contribution Dilemma

How does one ever decide how to divide charitable contributions? There are so many worthy causes, so many people in need, so many organizations that must have financial support to survive. I don't know about you, but I suffer a gigantic guilt trip every time I look at my checkbook and decide the till is far too empty to respond this month. With ceremony I tuck the appeal into a slot reserved exclusively for "worthy causes" and go about my day. Once such a decision to defer has been made I can forget the pangs — well, almost. This calm does not last long — oh, about as long as it takes the mailman to come back with another batch of "We need your help."

There seems no easy way out of it. I have attempted to set aside a certain amount each month to "give," but those who know me realize that simply would not work the way I balance my books. I rationalize need. Certainly we must give more than lip service to the religion we believe to be the right one for us. That concept was well-instilled in me by a fervently dedicated mother. There are groups who care for the less fortunate — missionaries, doctors, nurses, social workers; there are civic, social and benevolent groups who aspire to better the world around us; there are cultural organizations, libraries, art galleries, symphony orchestras and then the councils and commissions supporting a cause. How in the world can you contribute to each and feel you have adequately done your part?

There seem to be two schools of thought. Give a mite to each or choose one or two and go all out. Even this kind of decision defeats me. So let me tell you how I am, at the moment, handling my dilemma.

The moment an appeal arrives is the moment of decision in my case. If I feel affluent, I write a check. If the month is too young and routine payments still outstanding, too bad. Into the wastebasket it goes. Not that this operation is easy. I still feel I would like to reach out and say, "Gee, I'm sorry. Perhaps next time."

Perhaps I delude myself, but I keep having a nagging thought about gifts, tithing and charitable contributions. Is there not something to be said for "giving of one's self"? Isn't it possible to offer personal help to someone less fortunate, can't we do some necessary chores around a place that houses an interesting cause or can't we spend a few hours a week helping out at an office that sends notices to us and to which we feel sympathetic? It comes down to volunteerism, I guess—but man or woman hours that might otherwise cost money should not be overlooked.

Nor is it always the vast amount of giving that matters. In fact, if we all gave—just a little—it would amount to an impressive sum. The widow's mite, something she could ill afford to give, is important. This is something we might remember when we feel the paltry amount we give is not enough. Giving is the American way and we are a generous people. I guess the thing is to do what we can and be content with the ability to do that!

Smells That Make Me Remember

I doubt that others are as sensitive to smell as I am — oh, I don't mean things like rotten eggs or dead fish and the like. I mean smells that remind me of places and things — and people.

When my late husband came courting — and that is just over half a century ago — he had a very particular smell that I loved because, of course, it reminded me of him. He smoked — a dumb habit that all the young men simply HAD to do then. He drove a truck and worked on it where there was oil, gasoline and some grease, I guess. Well, he had a rather nice suede jacket that made him look very dapper. The smoke and garage smells were so worked into that animal hide that it carried Bernie's particular odor until the day it was discarded — completely in rags. I know because I carved up the back and sleeves to patch my little boy's pants (knees take a real beating from games of marbles).

Now and then, as I ride through the countryside on a foggy day, I smell Ireland. Burning turf (or peat) is a distinctive odor; and if you have a yen for the ol' sod as I do, you'll want to drop everything and take the next Aer Lingus plane out of Boston. Then there is a certain combination of cigarette smoke and Jameson's whiskey that reminds me of a small pub near Bunratty Castle. It's called "Dirty Nellie's"; but aye, it's a wonderful place.

There are lovely smells like the smell of sweet grass, from which the Penobscot Indians make baskets. Let one of them sit near an open window or drop into the water and the room is filled with a delicate aroma that is so fresh and clean. Bread baking or coffee perking are two more fresh smells. No matter how delicious food is, it is never as tantalizing as the smell.

Flowers are wonderful. My favorites are a single rose, or a small clump of lavender or lilies of the valley. The elusive sweetness that you must breath in deeply to savor is priceless beyond the most costly perfume. But carnations are not for me. Even a small bouquet is too funereal to please my nostrils.

The same can be said about heavy-scented soaps or great draughts of perfume. I find them offensive and often catch my breath because they are so overpowering. I say that the natural "earthy" smell of the barnyard or a farmer working in his hayfield is far more appealing than a person doused in ointments, powders and balms. Doesn't sound too feminine of me? Well, perhaps not, but that's the way I see it — or should I say SMELL it?

My mother often twitted me about having too acute a sense of smell and I guess she was right. She added that I was also a little too outspoken about her feminine toilette. She adored perfume. If I thought it was too overpowering, I rode in the car with the window open. We had more than a few amiable squabbles over that situation.

Today found a small letter of condolence from a young lady called Mary Lou who was very fond of Mom. In it, Mary Lou spoke of many things about Mom that she would always remember, and among them was: "Aunt Bessie always had such a lovely, delicate smell." What a simple thing — but how nice to be so remembered.

Affordable Art

Jim Perry (no relation) is a tall, taciturn man who left corporate America 20 years ago. He spent a full year weighing his future and where he wanted to be when retirement time arrived. A latent interest in art and a desire to become an artist settled the matter. He engaged carpenters to build a structure on land he owned just over the Chelsea line in Augusta. He designed the building and named it "The Talent Tree".

Now Jim and his able assistant, Joan Lathe, have all the work they can keep up with. They frame art heirlooms, they reconstruct damaged works of art, they arrange shows of many fine painters in Maine and surrounding states, and they sell art.

Jim is convinced art is a most marketable commodity if handled correctly. "Fine art should be as available to young families as a refrigerator or a stereo system. In fact, an electronic system purchased this year will undoubtedly be obsolete in three years. Works of art, on the other hand, will increase in value if kept intact. It also, I dare say, provides the family a great deal of pleasure along the way."

Jim believes art is being sorely overlooked as a business. He is willing to put his trust in people who want to own art, and has set up an installment plan or purchase to carry out his belief. "I feel even people on fixed incomes should be able to own and enjoy a piece of art being created today by Maine's terribly exciting artists," Jim said.

"I have the perfect business for me," he explained in a recent interview. "I wish every person might be able to enjoy life-after-retirement as much as I do." Everyone can afford to own art—at least that's how Jim Perry feels.

A New England study is underway to determine the impact nonprofit organizations have on a state's economy. Alden Wilson, Commissioner of the Maine Art Commission, refers to a ten-year-old report when he says, "Nonprofit arts [including museums, galleries and historic organizations] contribute more than $30,000,000 to Maine's economy." The current survey results reveal how close to the mark Wilson comes.

Long before such surveys were considered, in fact nearly 20 years ago, Jim Perry had the same belief. Jim has been offering original art by some of Maine's most prestigious artists on an installment plan. Such a conviction on the part of a businessman demonstrates the lengths he will go to make an attractive painting available to the art lover who would otherwise resort to less artistic decor.

The Talent Tree on outer Hospital Street in Augusta (Route 9) houses Jim Perry's gallery and laboratory, where he and his assistant restore and frame works of art. The gallery has a continuous show of works from which the public can purchase a chosen piece. The process is simple.

Once a piece is selected, Jim will quote the price and break it down to monthly payments. The only stipulation is that tax on the work must be paid up front before the transaction is undertaken. From that point on, the buyer has only to send a monthly check. Arrangements can usually be made to take the work home after a reasonable portion of the cost has been made. It's meaningful to note that a work selling for $150 can be yours for as little as $5.03 paid monthly over a three-year period. This cost includes a minimal interest charge — something almost every family could afford.

Jim and Joan make a real effort to hang a new show every month, but for a two-person operation sometimes this is a difficult arrangement. However, 19th-century art, contemporary work and some interesting sculpture is always available to view. Prices range from $150 to $10,000. Talent Tree hours are Monday through Friday 9 to 5:30 and Saturday 9 to 1. Special shows are announced in local papers.

A Number of Things

It surprises me to learn that something taking place in our area, and that is very important to me, is not even known about by my friends. Like Morning Pro Musica. A conversation with Jane went something like this —

"I wake up with the birds and Robert J. every morning!"

"Who in the world is Robert J., Katy?"

"Robert J. Lurtsimer on Maine Public Broadcasting Network."

"Never heard of him!"

Perhaps you have never heard of Robert J. or Will Curtis or Rachel Broemer of All Things Considered; but if you read the **Kennebec Observer** regularly, I bet you DO know something of Jeanette Cakouros. If you listen to "Maine Things Considered" at 5:30 every afternoon on 90.1 or 90.3 on FM **RADIO** (that's radio—turn off the television to catch this program) you can hear Jeannette read her monologues; they are great, very Maine and almost always something you can connect with.

Some dozen years ago I broadcast on WRDO radio from the old Augusta House and then from a corner of the dining room at Holiday Inn, so it is little wonder that radio is an important part of my day. It is my belief that public radio should be a part of your day too. There are many programs, such as the afternoon concerts, and you might not take to them right off; but there is some exciting programming and something for every member of the family.

I especially enjoy the "Radio Reader". Dick Estelle has a fine reading voice and I "know" some of the great books he has read to me as I drive up and down Maine highways. Catch him at 1-1:30 each afternoon. It takes several weeks, of course, for him to finish a book; but I often go the local library and read the chapters I missed, or finish the book if he lost me along the way. Super way to be entertained. This program is especially rewarding to people confined to their homes or (perish the thought) their beds.

It must have been eight or nine years ago when I met Garrison Keillor via MPBN. "Prairie Home Companion" was a Saturday evening MUST at my house. My U.S. Navy son was moving back east from his Oak Harbor, Washington tour of duty and was spending time in Maine before settling in the Boston area. His wife and children and I turned on the program at 6 o'clock, and knew Pete was catching the same folksy program as he drove up the pike to be home with us over the weekend. The program, I know, will be a happy memory for David and Meredith as they grow into adulthood—part of their Maine and Grandmother connection.

When I began this piece from my mental pickings, there were other surprises I was going to mention; but as is often the case, MPBN, its personalities and offerings pushed everything else aside. I'll elaborate another time, but let me close with a childhood memory. The very first song I ever learned in school, so many years ago, offers a thought that has stayed with me all these years.

"The world is so full of a number of things, I'm sure we should all be happy as kings." And indeed, we should be. Add to that sage thought that many of those "things" are free; and honestly, are not there more things to be happy about than unhappy?